PRINCES OF EUROPE

Torn between love and royal obligation...
by Rebecca Winters

Vincenzo and Valentino are determined to
fulfil their duty to their beloved kingdoms by taking
royal wives, but they haven't counted on
the revolutions taking place in their hearts caused by
two captivating commoners.

When these two charming Princes risk everything
to win the trust of the women they love they soon
find the true meaning of commitment and honour,
proving that sometimes fairytales do come true—
and in the most unexpected ways!

EXPECTING THE PRINCE'S BABY
Available in May 2014

and

BECOMING THE PRINCE'S WIFE
Available in June 2014

Dear Reader

BECOMING THE PRINCE'S WIFE is the second story in my two-book royal duet series. But Crown Prince Valentino of the Kingdom of Gemelli—destined to be King—isn't your usual prince. He has an unusual occupation besides running the affairs of his country.

His work captures the interest and imagination of my adventurous heroine Carolina, who hasn't allowed herself to get involved with any man because of a past tragedy. In theory, both of these exciting people are forbidden to each other, for several reasons, but when they're caught on fire by the same flame igniting them there's an explosion that changes destiny for both of them.

Enjoy their journey!

Rebecca Winters

BECOMING THE PRINCE'S WIFE

BY
REBECCA WINTERS

Published in Great Britain 2014
by Mills & Boon, an imprint of Harlequin (UK) Limited,
Eton House, 18-24 Paradise Road, Richmond, Surrey, TW9 1SR

© 2014 Rebecca Winters

ISBN: 978 0 263 24244 7

Harlequin (UK) policy is to use papers that are natural,
renewable and recyclable products and made from wood grown in
sustainable forests. The logging and manufacturing processes conform
to the legal environmental regulations of the country of origin.

Printed and bound in Spain
by CPI Antony Rowe, Chippenham, Wiltshire

Rebecca Winters, whose family of four children has now swelled to include five beautiful grandchildren, lives in Salt Lake City, Utah, in the land of the Rocky Mountains. With canyons and high alpine meadows full of wildflowers, she never runs out of places to explore. They, plus her favourite vacation spots in Europe, often end up as backgrounds for her romance novels, because writing is her passion, along with her family and church.

Rebecca loves to hear from readers. If you wish to e-mail her, please visit her website: www.cleanromances.com

Recent books by Rebecca Winters:

EXPECTING THE PRINCE'S BABY†
THE GREEK'S TINY MIRACLE
MARRY ME UNDER THE MISTLETOE**
A MARRIAGE MADE IN ITALY
ALONG CAME TWINS…*
BABY OUT OF THE BLUE*
THE COUNT'S CHRISTMAS BABY
THE RANCHER'S HOUSEKEEPER
A BRIDE FOR THE ISLAND PRINCE
SNOWBOUND WITH HER HERO

*Tiny Miracles
**Gingerbread Girls
†Princes of Europe

To my four wonderful, outstanding children:
Bill, John, Dominique and Max.

They've had to put up with a mother whose mind
is constantly dreaming up new fairytales
like the one I've just written.

Their unqualified love and constant support
has been the greatest blessing in my life.

CHAPTER ONE

As Carolena Baretti stepped out of the limousine, she could see her best friend, Abby, climbing the stairs of the royal jet. At the top she turned. "Oh, good! You're here!" she called to her, but was struggling to keep her baby from squirming out of her arms.

At eight months of age, little black-haired Prince Maximilliano, the image of his father, Crown Prince Vincenzo Di Laurentis of Arancia, was becoming big Max, fascinated by sights and sounds. Since he was teething, Carolena had brought him various colored toys in the shape of donuts to bite on. She'd give them to him after they'd boarded the jet for the flight to Gemelli.

The steward brought Carolena's suitcase on board while she entered the creamy interior of the jet. The baby's carryall was strapped to one of the luxury leather chairs along the side. Max fought at leaving his mother's arms, but she finally prevailed in getting him fastened down.

Carolena pulled a blue donut from the sack in her large straw purse. "Maybe this will help." She leaned over the baby and handed it to him. "What do you think, sweetheart?"

Max grabbed for it immediately and put it in his mouth to test it, causing both women to laugh. Abby gave her a hug. "Thank you for the gift. Any distraction is a blessing! The only time he doesn't move is when he's asleep."

Carolena chuckled.

"So you won't get too bored, I brought a movie for you to watch while we fly down. Remember I told you how much I loved the French actor Louis Jourdan when I was growing up?"

"He was in *Gigi,* right?"

"Yes, well, I found a movie of his in my mother's collection. You know me and my love for old films. This one is called *Bird of Paradise.* Since we'll be passing Mount Etna, I think you'll love it."

"I've never heard of that movie, but thank you for being so thoughtful. I'm sure I'll enjoy it."

"Carolena—I know this is a hard time for you, but I'm so glad you decided to come. Vincenzo and Valentino need to discuss business on this short trip. It will give you and me some time to do whatever we want while Queen Bianca dotes on her grandson."

"When Max smiles, I see traces of Michelina. That must delight her."

"I know it does. These days it's hard to believe Bianca was ever upset over the pregnancy. She's much warmer to me now."

"Thank heaven for that, Abby."

"You'll never know."

No, Carolena supposed she wouldn't. Not really. Abby Loretto had offered to be a surrogate mother to carry Their Highnesses' baby, but they'd both been through a trial by fire when Michelina was suddenly killed.

Carolena was thrilled for the two of them who, since that time, had fallen deeply in love and weathered the storm before marrying. Now they had a beautiful baby boy to raise and she was glad to have been invited to join them for their brief holiday.

Today was June fourth, a date she'd dreaded every June for the past seven years. It marked the death of her fiancé, Berto, and brought back horrendous guilt. She and Berto had shared a great love, but it had come to a tragic end too soon. All because of Carolena.

She'd been too adventurous for her own good, as her own wonderful, deceased grandmother had always told her. *You go where angels fear to tread without thinking of anyone but yourself. It's probably because you lost your parents too soon and I've failed you. One day there'll be a price to pay for being so headstrong.*

Tears stung her eyelids. How true were those words.

Berto's death had brought about a permanent change in Carolena. Outside of her professional work as an attorney, she never wanted to be responsible for another human life again. Though she'd dated a lot of men, her relationships were of short duration and superficial. After seven years, her pattern of noncommitment had become her way of life. No one depended on her. Her actions could affect no one or hurt anyone. That was the way she liked it.

Dear sweet Abby had known the date was coming up. Out of the goodness of her heart she'd insisted Carolena come with them on this trip so she wouldn't brood. Carolena loved her blonde friend for so many reasons, especially her thoughtfulness because she knew this time was always difficult for her.

As she strapped herself in, several bodyguards entered the body of the jet followed by black-haired Vincenzo. He stopped to give his wife and son a kiss before hugging Carolena. "It's good to see you. Gemelli is a beautiful country. You're going to love it."

"I'm sure I will. Thank you for inviting me, Vincenzo."

"Our pleasure, believe me. If you're ready, then we'll take off. I told Valentino we'd be there midafternoon."

Once he'd fastened himself in and turned to Abby with an eagerness Carolena could see and feel, the jet taxied to the runway. When it took off into a blue sky, it left the Principality of Arancia behind, a country nestled along the Riviera between France and Italy.

Before heading south, she could see the coastal waters of the Mediterranean receding, but it was obvious Abby and Vincenzo only had eyes for each other. Theirs was a true love story. Watching them was painful. There were moments like now when twenty-seven-year-old Carolena felt old before her time.

Thank goodness she had a movie to watch that she hadn't seen before. The minute it started she blinked at the sight of how young Louis Jourdan was. The story turned out to be about a Frenchman who traveled to Polynesia and fell in love with a native girl.

Carolena found herself riveted when the volcano erupts on the island and the native girl has to be sacrificed to appease the gods by jumping into it. The credits said the film had been made on location in Hawaii and used the Kilauea volcano for the scenes.

As the royal jet started to make its descent to Gemelli, she saw smoke coming out of Mount Etna, one of Italy's volcanoes. After watching this film, the thought of it erupting made her shiver.

The helicopter flew away from the new hot fumarole in the western pit of the Bocca Nuova of Mount Etna. The fumarole was a hole that let out gas and steam. After the scientific team had observed an increased bluish degassing from a vent in the saddle, they sent back video and seismic records before heading to the National Center of Geophysics and Volcanology lab in Catania on the eastern coast of Sicily.

En route to the lab the three men heard deep-seated explosions coming from inside the northeast crater, but there was no cause for public alarm in terms of evacuation alerts.

Once the center's helicopter touched ground, Crown Prince Valentino waved off his two colleagues and hurried to the royal helicopter for the short flight to Gemelli in the Ionian Sea. Their team had gotten back late, but they'd needed to do an in-depth study before transmitting vital data and photos.

Valentino's brother-in-law, Crown Prince Vincenzo Di Laurentis, along with his new wife, Abby, and son, Max, would already have been at the palace several hours. They'd come for a visit from Arancia and would be staying a few days. Valentino was eager to see them.

He and Vincenzo, distant cousins, had done shipping business together for many years but had grown closer with Vincenzo's first marriage to Michelina, who'd been Valentino's only sister. Her death February before last had left a hole in his heart. He'd always been very attached to his sibling and they'd confided in each other.

With his younger brother Vitale, nicknamed Vito, away in the military, Valentino had needed an outlet since her death. Lately, after a long day's work, he'd spent time quietly partying with a few good friends and his most recent girlfriend, while his mother, Bianca, the ruling Queen of Gemelli, occupied herself with their country's business.

As for tonight, he was looking forward to seeing Vincenzo as his helicopter ferried him to the grounds, where it landed at the rear of the sixteenth-century baroque palace. He jumped out and hurried past the gardens and tennis courts, taking a shortcut near the swimming pool to reach his apartment in the east wing.

But suddenly he saw something out of the corner of his eye that stopped him dead in his tracks. Standing on the end of the diving board ready to dive was a gorgeous, voluptuous woman in a knockout, fashionable one-piece purple swimsuit with a plunging neckline.

It was just a moment before she disappeared under the water, but long enough for him to forget the fiery fumarole on Mount Etna and follow those long legs to the end of the pool. When she emerged at the deep end with a sable-colored braid over one shoulder, he hunkered down to meet her. With eyes as sparkling green as lime zest, and a mouth with a passionate flare, she was even more breathtaking up close.

"Oh— Your Highness! I didn't think anyone was here!"

He couldn't have met her before or he would have remembered, because she would be impossible to forget. There was no ring on her finger. "You have me at a disadvantage, *signorina*."

She hugged her body close to the edge of the tiled pool. He got the impression she was trying to prevent him from getting the full view of her. That small show of modesty intrigued him.

"I'm Carolena Baretti, Abby Loretto's friend."

This woman was Abby's best friend? He'd heard Abby mention her, but Vincenzo had never said anything. Valentino knew his brother-in-law wasn't blind... Though they hadn't told him they were bringing someone else with them, he didn't mind. Not at all.

"How long have you been here?"

"We flew in at two o'clock. Right now the queen is playing with Max while Abby and Valentino take a nap." A nap, was it? He smiled inwardly. "So I decided to come out here for a swim. The air is like velvet."

He agreed. "My work took longer than I thought, making it impossible for me to be here when you arrived. I've planned a supper for us in the private dining room tonight. Shall we say half an hour? One of the staff will show you the way."

"That's very gracious of you, but I don't want to intrude on your time with them. I had a light meal before I came out to swim and I'll just go on enjoying myself here."

He got the sense she meant it. The fact that she wasn't being coy like so many females he'd met in his life aroused his interest. "You're their friend, so it goes without saying you're invited." His lips broke into a smile. "And even if you weren't with them, I *like* an intrusion as pleasant as this one. I insist you join us."

"Thank you," she said quietly, but he had an idea she was debating whether or not to accept his invitation, mystifying him further. "Before you go, may I say how sorry I am about the loss of Princess Michelina. I can see the resemblance to your sister in you and the baby. I know it's been devastating for your family, especially the queen. But if anyone can instill some joy into all of you, it's your adorable nephew, Max."

The surprises just kept coming. Valentino was taken aback. The fact that she'd been in Abby's confidence for a number of years had lent a sincere ring to this woman's remarks, already putting them on a more intimate footing. "I've been eager to see him again. He's probably grown a foot since last time."

An engaging smile appeared. "Maybe not quite another foot yet, but considering he's Prince Vincenzo's son, I would imagine he'll be tall one day."

"That wouldn't surprise me. *A presto,* Signorina Baretti."

Carolena watched *his* tall physique stride to the patio and disappear inside a set of glass doors. Long after he'd left, she was still trying to catch her breath. When she'd broken the surface of the water at the other end of the rectangular pool, she'd recognized the striking thirty-two-year-old crown prince right away.

Her knowledge of him came from newspapers and television that covered the funeral of his sister, Princess Michelina. He'd ridden in the black-and-gold carriage with his brother and their mother, Queen Bianca, the three of them grave and in deep grief.

In a recent poll he'd been touted the world's most sought-after royal bachelor. Most of the tabloids revealed he went through women like water. She could believe it. Just now his eyes had mirrored his masculine admiration of her. Everywhere they roved, she'd felt heat trail over her skin. By that invisible process called osmosis, his charm and sophistication had managed to seep into her body.

But even up close no camera could catch the startling midnight blue of his dark-lashed eyes. The dying rays of the evening sun gilded the tips of his medium cut dark blond hair and brought out his hard-boned facial features, reminiscent of his Sicilian ancestry. He was a fabulous-looking man.

Right then he'd been wearing jeans that molded his powerful thighs, and a white shirt with the sleeves shoved up to the elbows to reveal hard-muscled forearms. No sign of a uniform this evening.

Whatever kind of work he did, he'd gotten dirty. She wondered where he'd been. There were black marks on his clothes and arms, even on his face, bronzed from being outdoors. If anything, the signs of the working man intensified his potent male charisma. He wasn't just a handsome prince without substance.

Carolena was stunned by her reaction to him. There'd been many different types of men who'd come into her life because of her work as an attorney; businessmen, manufacturers, technology wizards, mining engineers, entrepreneurs. But she had to admit she'd never had this kind of visceral response to a man on a first meeting, not even with Berto, who'd been her childhood friend before they'd fallen in love.

The prince had said half an hour. Carolena hadn't intended to join the three of them this evening, but since he'd used the word *insist,* she decided she'd better go so as not to offend him. Unfortunately it was growing late. She needed to hurry inside and get ready, but she wouldn't have time to wash her hair.

She climbed out of the pool and retraced her steps to the other wing of the palace. After a quick shower, she unbraided her hair and swept it back with an amber comb. Once she'd applied her makeup, she donned a small leopard-print wrap dress with ruched elbow-length sleeves. The tiny amber stones of her chandelier earrings matched the ones in her small gold chain necklace. On her feet she wore designer wedges in brown and amber.

The law firm in Arancia where she worked demanded their attorneys wear designer clothes since they dealt with an upper-class clientele. Abby had worked there with her until her fifth month of pregnancy when she'd been forced to quit. After being employed there twenty months and paid a generous salary, Carolena had accumulated a wonderful wardrobe and didn't need to worry she wouldn't have something appropriate to wear to this evening's dinner.

A knock at the door meant a maid was ready to take her to the dining room. But when she opened it, she received another shock to discover the prince at the threshold wearing a silky charcoal-brown sport shirt and beige trousers.

He must not have trusted her to come on her own. She didn't know whether to be flattered or worried she'd made some kind of faux pas when she'd declined his invitation at first. Their eyes traveled over each other. A shower had gotten rid of the black marks. He smelled wonderful, no doubt from the soap he used. Her heart did a tiny thump before she got hold of herself.

"Your Highness— This is the second time you've surprised me this evening."

He flashed her a white smile. "Unexpected surprises make life more interesting, don't you think?"

"I do actually, depending on the kind."

"This was the kind I couldn't resist."

Obviously she *had* irritated him. Still, she couldn't believe he'd come to fetch her. "I'm honored to be personally escorted by none other than the prince himself."

"That wasn't so hard to say, was it?" His question brought a smile to her lips. "Since I'm hungry, I thought I'd accompany you to the dining room myself to hurry things up, and I must admit I'm glad you're ready."

"Then let's not waste any more time."

"Vincenzo and Abby are already there, but they didn't even notice me when I passed by the doors. I've heard of a honeymoon lasting a week or two, even lon-ger. But eight months?"

Carolena chuckled. "I know what you mean. While we were flying out, they were so caught up in each other, I don't think they said more than two words to me."

"Love should be like that, but it's rare."

"I know," she murmured. Vincenzo and Michelina hadn't enjoyed a marriage like that. It was no news to Carolena or Valentino, so they left the subject alone.

She followed him down several corridors lined with tapestries and paintings to a set of doors guarded by a staff member. They opened onto the grounds. "We'll cut across here past the gardens to the other wing of the palace. It's faster."

There was nothing stiff or arrogant about Prince Valentino. He had the rare gift of being able to put her at ease and make her feel comfortable.

She looked around her. "The gardens are glorious. You have grown a fabulous collection of palms and exotic plants. Everything thrives here. And I've never seen baroque architecture this flamboyant."

He nodded. "My brother, Vito, and I have always called it the Putti Palace because of all the winged boy cherubs supporting the dozens of balconies. To my mother's chagrin, we used to draw mustaches on them. For our penance, we had to wash them off."

Laughter rippled out of her. "I'm afraid to tell Abby what you said for fear she'll have nightmares over Max getting into mischief."

"Except that won't be for a while yet." His dark blue

eyes danced. No doubt this prince had been a handful to his parents. Somehow the thought made him even more approachable.

"With all these wrought-iron balustrades and rustication, the palace really is beautiful."

"Along with the two-toned lava masonry, the place is definitely unique," he commented before ushering her through another pair of doors, where a staff member was on duty. Their arms brushed in the process, sending little trickles of delight through her body. Her reaction was ridiculous. It had to be because she'd never been this close to a prince before. Except for Vincenzo, of course, but he didn't count. Not in the same way.

They walked down one more hall to the entrance of the dining room where Abby and Vincenzo sat at the candlelit table with their heads together talking quietly and kissing. Gilt-framed rococo mirrors made the room seem larger, projecting their image.

Valentino cleared his throat. "Should we come back?" He'd already helped Carolena to be seated. The teasing sound in his voice amused her, but his question caused the other two to break apart. While Abby's face flushed, Vincenzo got to his feet and came around to give Valentino a hug.

"It's good to see you."

"Likewise. I'm sorry I took so long. It's my fault for leaving work late today, but it couldn't be helped."

"No one understands that better than I do. We took the liberty of bringing Carolena with us. Allow me to introduce you."

Valentino shot her a penetrating glance. "We already met at the swimming pool."

Carolena felt feverish as she and Abby exchanged a silent glance before he walked around to hug her friend. Then he took his place next to Carolena, who still hadn't recovered from her initial reaction to his masculine appeal.

In a moment, dinner was served, starting with deep-fried risotto croquettes stuffed with pistachio pesto called arancini because they were the shape and size of an orange. Pasta with clams followed called spaghetti alle vongole. Then came the main course of crab and an aubergine side dish. Valentino told them the white wine came from their own palace vineyard.

"The food is out of this world, but I'll have to pass on the cannoli dessert," Carolena exclaimed a little while later. "If I lived here very long I'd look like one of those fat Sicilian rock partridges unable to move around."

Both men burst into laughter before Valentino devoured his dessert.

Carolena looked at Abby. "What did I say?"

Vincenzo grinned. "You and my wife have the same thought processes. She was afraid pregnancy would make her look like a beached whale."

"We women have our fears," Abby defended.

"We certainly do!"

Valentino darted Carolena another glance. "In that purple swimsuit you were wearing earlier, I can guarantee you'll never have that problem."

She'd walked into that one and felt the blood rush to her cheeks. That suit was a frivolous purchase she wouldn't have worn around other people, but since she'd been alone... Or so she'd thought. "I hope you're right, Your Highness."

His eyes smiled. "Call me Val."

Val? Who in the world called him that?

He must have been able to read her mind because his next comment answered her question. "My brother and I didn't like our long names, so we gave ourselves nicknames. He's Vito and I'm Val."

"V and V," she said playfully. "I'm surprised you didn't have to wash your initials off some of those putti."

Another burst of rich laughter escaped his throat. When it subsided, he explained their little joke to Vincenzo and Abby.

Carolena smiled at Abby. "I'd caution you never to tell that story to Max, or when he's more grown up he might take it into his head to copy his uncles."

"Fortunately we don't have putti," Vincenzo quipped.

"True," Abby chimed in, "but we do have busts that can be knocked over by a soccer ball."

Amidst the laughter, a maid appeared in the doorway. "Forgive the intrusion, Your Highness, but the queen says it seems the young prince has started to cry and is running a temperature."

In an instant both parents jumped to their feet bringing an end to the frivolity.

Wanting to say something to assure them, Carolena said, "He's probably caught a little cold."

Abby nodded. "I'm sure you're right, but he's still not as used to the queen yet and is in a strange place. I'll go to him." She put a hand on Vincenzo's arm. "You stay here and enjoy your visit, darling."

At this point, Valentino stood up. "We'll have all day tomorrow. Right now your boy needs both of you."

"Thank you," they murmured. Abby came around to give Carolena a hug. "See you in the morning."

"Of course. If you need me for anything, just phone me."

"I will."

When they disappeared out the doors, Carolena got to her feet. "I'll say good-night, too. Thank you for a wonderful dinner, Your Highness."

He frowned. "The name's Val. I want to hear you say it."

She took a deep breath. "Thank you...Val."

"That's better." His gaze swept over her. "Where's the fire?"

"I'm tired." Carolena said the first thing that came into her head. "I was up early to finish some work at the firm before the limo arrived to drive me to the airport. Bed sounds good to me."

"Then I'll walk you back."

"That won't be necessary."

He cocked his dark blond head. "Do I frighten you?"

Your appeal frightens me. "If anything, I'm afraid of disturbing your routine."

"I don't have one tonight. Forget I'm the prince."

It wasn't the prince part that worried her. He'd made her aware of him as a man. This hadn't happened since she'd fallen in love with Berto and it was very disturbing to her.

"To be honest, when you showed up at the swimming pool earlier, you looked tired after a hard day's work. Since it's late, I'm sure you'd like a good sleep before you spend the day with Vincenzo tomorrow."

"I'm not too tired to see you back to your room safely."

"Your Highness?" The same maid came to the entrance once more. "The queen would like to see you in her apartment."

"I'll go to her. Thank you."

He cupped Carolena's elbow to walk her out of the dining room. She didn't want him touching her. The contact made her senses come alive. When they passed the guard and reached the grounds, she eased away from him.

"After getting to know Vincenzo, I realize how busy you are and the huge amount of calls on your time. Your mother is waiting for you."

"I always say good-night to my mother before retiring. If our dinner had lasted a longer time, she would have had a longer wait."

There was no talking him out of letting her get back to her room by herself. "What kind of work were you doing today?" She had to admit to a deep curiosity.

He grinned. "I always come home looking dirty and need to wash off the grime."

She shook her head. "I didn't say that."

"You didn't have to. Volcanoes are a dirty business."

Carolena came to a standstill before lifting her head to look at him. "You were up on Mount Etna?"

"That's right."

His answer perplexed her. "Why?"

"I'm a volcanologist with the National Center of Geophysics and Volcanology lab in Catania."

"You're kidding—" After that movie she'd watched on the plane, she couldn't believe what he'd just told her.

One corner of his compelling mouth lifted. "Even a prince can't afford to be an empty suit. Etna has been my backyard since I was born. From the first moment I saw it smoking, I knew I had to go up there and get a good look. Once that happened, I was hooked."

With his adventurous spirit, she wasn't surprised but knew there was a lot more to his decision than that. "I confess it would be fantastic to see it up close the way you do. Have you been to other volcanoes?"

"Many of them."

"You lucky man! On the way down here I watched a Hollywood movie with Louis Jourdan about a volcano erupting in Polynesia."

"You must mean *Bird of Paradise.*"

"Yes. It was really something. Your line of work has to be very dangerous."

For a second she thought she saw a flicker of some emotion in his eyes, but it passed. "Not so much nowadays. The main goal is to learn how to predict trouble so that timely warnings can be issued for cautioning and evacuating people in the area. We've devised many safe ways to spy on active volcanoes over the decades."

"How did your parents feel about you becoming a volcanologist?"

A smile broke the corner of his mouth, as if her question had amused him. "When I explained the reasons for my interest, they approved."

That was too pat an answer. He sounded as if he wanted to get off the subject, but she couldn't let it go. "What argument did you give them?"

His brows lifted. "Did you think I needed one?"

She took a quick breath. "If they were anything like my grandmother, who was the soul of caution, then yes!"

He stopped outside the entrance to her wing of the palace. Moonlight bathed his striking male features, making them stand out like those of the Roman-god statues supporting the fountain in the distance. His sudden serious demeanor gave her more insight into his complex personality.

"A king's first allegiance is to the welfare of his people. I explained to my parents that when Etna erupts again, and she will, I don't want to see a repeat of what happened in 1669."

Carolena was transfixed. "What *did* happen?"

"That eruption turned into a disaster that killed over twenty-nine thousand people."

She shuddered, remembering the film. "I can't even imagine it."

He wore a grim expression. "Though it couldn't happen today, considering the sophisticated warning systems in place, people still need to be educated about the necessity of listening and heeding those warnings of evacuation."

"In the film, there'd been no warning."

"Certainly not a hundred years ago. That's been my

greatest concern. Gemelli has a population of two hundred thousand, so it can't absorb everyone fleeing the mainland around Catania, but I want us to be prepared as much as possible."

"How do you get your people prepared?"

"I've been working with our government to do mock drills to accommodate refugees from the mainland, should a disaster occur. Every ship, boat, barge, fishing boat would have to be available, not to mention housing and food and airlifts to other islands."

"That would be an enormous undertaking."

"You're right. For protection against volcanic ash and toxic gas, I've ordered every family outfitted with lightweight, disposable, filtering face-piece mask/respirators. This year's sightings have convinced me I've only scratched the surface of what's needed to be done to feel at all ready."

"Your country is very fortunate to have you for the watchman."

"The watchman? That makes me sound like an old sage."

"You're hardly old yet," she quipped.

"I'm glad you noticed." His remark caused her heart to thud for no good reason.

"I'm very impressed over what you do."

"It's only part of what I do."

"Oh, I know what a prince does." She half laughed. "Abby once read me Vincenzo's itinerary for the day and I almost passed out. But she never told me about *your* scientific background."

"It isn't something I talk about."

"Well, I think it's fascinating! You're likean astronaut or a test pilot, but the general population doesn't know what you go through or how you put your life on the line."

"That's a big exaggeration."

"Not at all," she argued. "It's almost as if you're leading a double life. What a mystery you are!"

She wouldn't have put it past Abby to have chosen that particular film because she knew about Valentino's profession and figured Carolena would get a kick out of it once she learned about his secret profession.

After a low chuckle, he opened the doors so they could walk down the hallway and around the corner to her room. She opened her door. Though she was dying to ask him a lot more questions about his work in volcanology, she didn't want him to think she expected his company any longer. She was also aware the queen was waiting for him.

"It's been a lovely evening. Thank you for everything."

His eyes gleamed in the semidarkness. "What else do you do besides give unsuspecting males a heart attack while you're diving?"

Heat scorched her cheeks. "I thought I was alone."

"Because I was late getting back, I cut through that part of the grounds and happened to see you. It looks like I'm going to have to do it more often."

He was a huge flirt. The tabloids hadn't been wrong about him. "I won't be here long enough to get caught again. I have a law practice waiting for me back in Arancia."

He studied her for a moment. "I heard you're in the same firm with Abby."

"We were until her marriage. Now she's a full-time mother to your nephew."

A heart-stopping smile appeared. "It must be tough on your male colleagues working around so much beauty and brains."

"They're all married."

"That makes it so much worse."

She laughed. "You're outrageous."

"Then we understand each other. Tomorrow we'll be eating breakfast on the terrace off the morning room. I'll send a maid for you at eight-thirty. *Buona notte, Carolena.*"

"Buona notte."

"Val," he said again.

"Val," she whispered before shutting the door. She lay against it, surprised he was so insistent on her using his nickname, surprised he'd made such an impact on her.

After their delicious meal, she wasn't ready for bed yet. Once she'd slipped on her small garden-print capri pajamas, she set up her laptop on the table and started to look up Mount Etna. The amount of information she found staggered her. There were dozens of videos and video clips she watched until after one in the morning.

But by the time she'd seen a video about six volcanologists killed on the Galeras volcano in the Colombian Andes in 1993, she turned off her computer. The scientists had been standing on the ground when it began to heave and then there was a deafening roar. The volcano exploded, throwing boulders and ash miles high and they'd lost their lives.

The idea of that happening to the prince made her ill. She knew he took precautions, but as he'd pointed out, there was always a certain amount of risk. The desire to see a vent up close would be hard to resist. That's what he did in his work. He crept up close to view the activity and send back information. But there might come a day when he'd be caught. She couldn't bear the thought of it, but she admired him terribly.

The playboy prince who'd had dozens of girlfriends didn't mesh with the volcanologist whose name was Val. She didn't want to care about either image of the sensational-looking flesh-and-blood man. When Carolena finally pulled the covers over her, she fell asleep wishing she'd never met him. He was too intriguing for words.

At seven-thirty the next morning her cell phone rang, causing her to wonder if it was the prince. She got a fluttery feeling in her chest as she raised up on one elbow to reach for it. To her surprise it was Abby and she clicked on. "Abby? Are you all right? How's Max?"

"He's still running a temperature and fussing. I think he's cutting another tooth. The reason I'm calling is because I'm going to miss breakfast with you and stay in the apartment with him. It will give Vincenzo and Valentino time to get some work done this morning."

"Understood. I'm so sorry Max is sick."

"It'll pass, but under the circumstances, why don't you order breakfast in your room or out by the pool. I'll get in touch with you later in the day. If you want a limo, just dial zero and ask for one to drive you into town, and do a little shopping or something."

"Don't worry about me. I'll love relaxing by the pool. This is heaven after the hectic schedule at the law firm."

"Okay, then. Talk to you soon."

This was a good turn of events. The less she saw of Valentino, the better.

CHAPTER TWO

BY TEN-THIRTY A.M., Valentino could see that Vincenzo wasn't able to concentrate. "Let's call it a day. I can see you want to be with Abby and Max. When I've finished with some other business, we'll meet for dinner."

Vincenzo nodded. "Sorry, Valentino."

"You can't help this. Family has to come first." He walked his brother-in-law out of his suite where they'd had breakfast while they talked. When they'd said goodbye, he closed the door, realizing he had a free day on his hands if he wanted it.

In truth, he'd never wanted anything more and walked over to the house phone to call Carolena Baretti's room, but there was no answer. He buzzed his assistant. "Paolo? Did Signorina Baretti go into town?"

"No. She had breakfast at the pool and is still there."

"I see. Thank you."

Within minutes he'd changed into trunks and made his way to the pool with a beach towel and his phone. He spotted her sitting alone reading a book under the shade of the table's umbrella. She'd put her hair in a braid and was wearing a lacy cover-up, but he could see a spring-green bikini beneath it.

"I guess it was too much to hope you were wearing that purple swimsuit I found you in last evening."

She looked up. Maybe it was a trick of light, but he thought she looked nervous to see him. Why?

Carolena put her book down. "You've finished your work with Vincenzo already?"

He tossed the towel on one of the other chairs. "Between you and me, I think he wanted to take a nap with his wife."

A smile appeared. "They deserve some vacation time away from deadlines."

"Amen. We'll do more work tomorrow when Max is feeling better. Come swim with me."

She shook her head. "I've already been in."

"There's no law that says you can't swim again, is there?" He put his phone on the table.

"No. Please—just forget I'm here."

"I'm afraid that would be impossible," he said over his shoulder before plunging in at the deep end to do some laps. When he eventually lifted his head, he was shocked to discover she'd left the patio and was walking back to her wing of the palace on those long shapely legs.

Nothing like this had ever happened to him before. Propelled into action, he grabbed his things and caught up to her as she was entering the door of her apartment. Valentino stood in the aperture so she couldn't close it on him.

"Did you go away because I'd disturbed you with

my presence? Or was it because you have an aversion to me, *signorina?*"

Color swept into her cheeks. "Neither one."

His adrenaline surged. "Why didn't you tell me you preferred to be alone?"

"I'm just a guest. You're the prince doing your own thing. This is your home. But I had no intention of offending you by leaving the pool."

He frowned. "Yesterday I asked if you were afraid of me. You said no, but I think you are and I want to know why. It's true that though I've been betrothed to Princess Alexandra for years, I've had a love life of sorts. In that way I'm no different than Vincenzo before he married Michelina. But I've the feeling Abby has painted me as such a bad boy to you, you're half terrified to be alone with me."

"Nothing of the sort, Your Highness!" She'd backed away from him. "Don't ever blame her for anything. She thinks the world of you!"

That sounded heartfelt. "Then invite me in so we can talk without the staff hearing every word of our conversation."

She bit her lip before standing aside so he could enter. "I'll get you a dry towel so you can sit down." He closed the door and watched her race through the suite. She soon came hurrying back with a towel and folded it on one of the chairs placed around the coffee table.

"Thank you," he said as she took a seat at the end of the couch.

He sat down with his hands clasped between his legs and stared at her. "What's wrong with you? Though

I've told you I find you attractive, it doesn't mean I'm ready to pounce on you." She averted her eyes. "Don't tell me you don't know what I'm talking about."

"I wasn't going to, and I didn't mean to be rude. You have to believe me."

She sounded sincere enough, but Valentino wasn't about to let her off the hook. "What else am I to think? Last night I thought we were enjoying each other's company while we talked, but today you act like a frightened schoolgirl. Has some man attacked you before? Is that the reason you like to be alone and ran the minute I dived into the water?"

Her head lifted. "No! You don't understand."

"Since you're a special guest, help me so I don't feel like some pariah."

"Forgive me if I made you feel that way." Her green orbs pleaded with him. "This has to do with me, not you."

"Are you this way on principle with every man you meet? Or am I the only one to receive that honor?"

She stood up. "I—I'm going through a difficult time right now." Her voice faltered. "It's something I really can't talk about. Could we start over again, as if this never happened?"

Much as he'd like to explore her problem further, he decided to let it rest for now. "That all depends." On impulse he said, "Do you like to ride horses?"

"I love it. I used to ride all the time on my grandparents' farm."

Good. "Then I'll have lunch sent to your room, and I'll collect you in an hour. We'll ride around the grounds. It's someplace safe and close to Abby, who's hoping you're having a good time. But if you're afraid of what happened to my sister while she was riding, we could play tennis."

"I'm not afraid, but to go riding must be a painful reminder to you."

"I've worked my way through it. Accidents can happen anytime. To worry about it unnecessarily takes away from the quality of life. Don't you think?"

Her eyes suddenly glistened. "Yes," she whispered with such deep emotion he was more curious than ever to know what was going on inside her, and found himself wanting to comfort her. Instead he had to tear himself away.

"I'll be back in an hour." Reaching for his towel and phone, he left the apartment and hurried through the palace to his suite. Maybe by the end of their ride today, he'd have answers...

Carolena stood in the living room surprised and touched by his decency. He'd thought she'd been assaulted by a man and wanted to show her she didn't need to be afraid of him while he entertained her. No doubt he felt an obligation to her with Vincenzo and Abby indisposed.

He was sensitive, too. How many men would have worried she might be afraid to ride after what had happened to his sister? She'd gotten killed out riding, but he didn't let that stop him from living his normal life. His concern for Carolena's feelings increased her admiration for him.

So far she'd been a perfectly horrid guest, while he

was going out of his way to make this trip eventful for her when he didn't have to. This wasn't the behavior of a playboy. The crown prince was proving to be the perfect host, increasing her guilt for having offended him.

Within the hour he came for her in a limo and they drove to the stables across the vast estate. Once he'd picked the right mare for her, they headed out to enjoy the scenery. In time, he led them through a heavily wooded area to a lake. They dismounted and walked down to the water's edge.

"What a beautiful setting."

"We open it to the public on certain days of the month."

"Abby used to tell me she felt like a princess in a fairy tale growing up on the palace grounds in Arancia. If I lived here, I'd feel exactly the same way. You and your siblings must have spent hours here when you were young." On impulse she asked, "Were they interested in volcanology, too?"

His eyes swerved to hers. She had the feeling she'd surprised him by her question. "Quite the opposite."

That sounded cryptic. "What's the real reason you developed such a keen interest? It isn't just because Etna is there."

"It's a long story." There was that nuance of sadness in his voice again.

"We've got the rest of the afternoon." She sank onto her knees in the lush grass facing the water where an abundance of waterfowl bobbed around. "Humor me. Last night I was up until one o'clock looking at video clips of Etna and other volcanoes. They were incredible. I really want to know what drove you to become so interested."

He got down on the grass next to her. "My father had a sibling, my uncle Stefano. He was the elder son and the crown prince, but he never wanted to be king. He fought with my grandfather who was then King of Gemelli.

"Uncle Stefano hated the idea of being betrothed and having to marry a woman picked out for him. Our country has never had a sovereign who wasn't married by the time he ascended the throne. It's the law. But Stefano didn't ever want to be king and left home at eighteen to travel the world. I knew he had various girlfriends, so he didn't lead a celibate life, but he never married.

"In time, volcanoes fascinated him and he decided he wanted to study them. To appease my grandparents, he came home occasionally to touch base. I was young and loved him because he was so intelligent and a wonderful teacher. He used to take me up on Etna.

"The day came when I decided I wanted to follow in his footsteps and announced I was going to attend the university to become a geologist. My parents could see my mind was made up.

"While I was at school, the family got word he'd been killed on the Galeras volcano in the Colombian Andes."

"Valentino—" she gasped. "I read about it on the website last night. One of the people killed was your uncle?"

Pain marred his striking male features. "He got too close. The ash and gas overpowered him and he died."

She shuddered. "That's horrible. I should have thought

it would have put you off wanting anything more to do with your studies."

"You might think it, but I loved what I was doing. Statistics prove that on average only one volcanologist dies on the job each year or so."

"That's one too many!"

"For our family it was traumatic because of the consequences that followed. His body was shipped home for the funeral. A few weeks later my grandfather suffered a fatal heart attack, no doubt from the shock. His death meant my father took over as king with my mother at his side.

"While we were still grieving, they called me into their bedroom and told me they were all right with my desire to be a volcanologist. But they prayed I wouldn't disappoint them the way my uncle had disappointed my grandfather. They said my uncle Stefano had disgraced the family by not taking up his royal duties and marrying.

"I was torn apart because I'd loved him and knew he'd suffered because he'd turned his back on his royal heritage. But when I heard my parents' sorrow, I promised I would fulfill my princely obligation to the crown and marry when the time was right. They wouldn't have to worry about me. Michelina and I made a pact that we'd always do our duty."

"You mean that if she'd wanted to marry someone else other than Vincenzo, she would still have done her duty."

He nodded. "I asked her about that, knowing Vincenzo didn't love her in the way she loved him. She said it didn't matter. She was committed and was hoping he'd fall in love with her one day."

"Did you resent him for not being able to love your sister?"

"How could I do that when I don't love Alexandra? When I saw how hard he tried to make Michelina happy by agreeing to go through the surrogacy process, my affection for him grew. He was willing to do anything to make their marriage better. Vincenzo is one of the finest men I've ever known. When he ended up marrying Abby, I was happy for him."

"You're a remarkable person. So was your sister."

"I loved her. She could have told our parents she refused to enter into a loveless marriage, but she didn't. Uncle Stefano's death had affected all of us, including our brother, Vito. One day after his military service is over, he, too, will have to marry royalty because he's second in line to the throne."

"The public has no idea of the anguish that goes on behind locked royal doors."

"We're just people who've been born to a strange destiny. I didn't want to disappoint my parents or be haunted with regrets like my uncle. Fortunately, Mother is still capable of ruling, and my time to fulfill my obligation hasn't come yet."

"But it will one day."

"Yes."

"It's hard to comprehend a life like yours. May I be blunt and ask you if you have a girlfriend right now?"

"I've been seeing someone in town."

She had to suppress a moan. *Did you hear that, Carolena?* "And she's all right with the situation?"

"Probably not, but from the beginning she's known we couldn't possibly have a future. In case you're wondering, I haven't slept with her."

Carolena shook her head. "You don't owe me any explanation."

"Nevertheless, I can see the next question in your eyes and so I'll answer it. Contrary to what the media says about me, there have been only a few women with whom I've had an intimate relationship, but they live outside the country."

"Yet knowing you are betrothed has never stopped any of them from wanting to spend time with you?"

"No. The women I've known haven't been looking for permanency, either." He smiled. "We're like those ships passing in the night."

It sounded awful. Yet, since Berto, she hadn't been looking for permanency, either, and could relate more than he knew.

"I've warned my latest girlfriend our relationship could end at any time. You're within your rights to condemn me, Carolena."

"I could never condemn you," she whispered, too consumed by guilt over how she'd accidentally brought out Berto's death to find fault with anyone. "You've had every right to live your life like any ordinary man. But like your uncle, it must have been brutal for you to have grown up knowing your bride was already chosen for you."

"I've tried not to think about it."

Her mind reeled from the revelations. "Does your betrothed know and understand?"

"I'm quite sure Princess Alexandra has had relationships, too. It's possible she's involved with someone she cares about right now. Her parents' expectations for her haven't spared her anguish, either."

"No," she murmured, but it was hard to understand. How could any man measure up to Valentino? If Princess Alexandra was like his sister, she'd been in love with Valentino for years. "Does she support your work as a volcanologist?"

"I haven't asked her."

"Why not?"

"Up to now we've been living our own lives apart as much as possible."

"But this is an integral part of your life!"

He sat up, chewing on the end of a blade of grass. "Our two families have spent occasional time together over the years. But the last time my brother was home on leave and went to Cyprus with me and my mother, he told me that Alexandra admitted she never liked the idea that I was a volcanologist."

"And that doesn't worry you?"

He studied her for a long moment. "It's an issue we'll have to deal with one day after we're married."

"By then it will be too late to work things out between you," she cried. "How often do you fly to Catania?"

"Four times a week."

"She's not going to like that, not if she hates the idea of it."

He gave her a compassionate smile. "Our marriage won't be taking place for a long time, so I choose not to worry about it."

"I don't see how you can stand it."

"You learn to stand it when you've been born into a royal family. Why fate put me in line for the throne instead of you, for example, I don't know."

"You mean a woman can rule?"

"If there are no other males. Under those circumstances, she must marry another royal so she can reign. But my grandparents didn't have a daughter. Uncle Stefano should have been king, but he rebelled, so it fell to my father to rule."

Tears trickled down her cheeks. "How sad for your uncle."

"A double sadness, because though he'd abdicated in order to choose his own life, he was burdened with the pain of disappointing his parents."

"There's been so much pain for all of you. And now your own sister and father have passed on."

He nodded. "It's life."

"But it's so much to handle." Her voice trembled. Carolena wanted to comfort him but realized no one could erase all that sadness. She wiped the moisture off her cheeks. "You didn't have to tell me anything. I feel honored that you did."

His gaze roved over her. "Your flattering interest in what I do prompted me to talk about something I've kept to myself for a long time. It felt good to talk about it. Why don't you try it out on me by telling me what's bothering you."

Her eyes closed tightly for a moment. "Let's just say someone that I loved died and it was my fault. Unlike you, I can't seem to move on from the past."

"Maybe you haven't had enough time to grieve."

Carolena could tell him seven years had been more than enough time to grieve. At this point, grief wasn't her problem. Guilt was the culprit. But all she said to him was, "Maybe."

"It might be therapeutic to confide in someone. Even me."

His sincerity warmed her heart, but confiding in him would be the worst thing she could do. To remain objective around him, she needed to keep some barriers between them. "You have enough problems."

"None right this minute."

He stared hard at her. "Was his death intentional?"

"No."

"I didn't think it was. Have you gone for counseling?"

"No. It wouldn't help."

"You don't know that."

"Yes, I do." In a panic, she started to get up. He helped her the rest of the way. "Thank you for being willing to listen." It was time to change the subject. "Your uncle would be so happy to see how he guided you on your particular path, and more especially on how you're putting that knowledge to exceptional use. If I'd had such an uncle, I would have made him take me with him, too. What you do can be dangerous, but it *is* thrilling."

"You're right about that," he said, still eyeing her

speculatively. "Shall we head out? By the time we reach the palace, hopefully Vincenzo will have good news for us about Max and we can all eat dinner together."

"I hope so."

They mounted their horses and took a different route to the stable. A limo was waiting to take them back to her wing of the palace. When they arrived, she opened the car door before he could. "You don't need to see me inside. Thank you for a wonderful day."

He studied her through veiled eyes. "It was my pleasure. I'll call you when I've spoken with Vincenzo."

She nodded before getting out of the limo. After hurrying inside, she took a quick shower, applied her makeup and arranged her hair in a loose knot on top of her head. For the first time in years her thoughts hadn't been on Berto. They'd been full of the prince, who'd brought her alive from the moment he'd appeared at the side of the pool.

No matter that he had a girlfriend at the moment, it was hard to breathe every time Carolena thought of the way he'd looked at her. She could understand why any woman lucky enough to catch his eye would be willing to stay in a relationship as long as possible to be with him. There was no one like him.

Needing to do something with all this energy he'd generated through no fault of his own, she got dressed, deciding to wear a short-sleeved crocheted lace top in the same egg shell color as her linen pants. The outfit was light and airy. She toned it with beige ankle-strap crisscross espadrilles.

While she was waiting for a phone call, she heard

a knock on the door and wondered if it might be the prince. With a pounding heart she reached for her straw bag and opened it, but it was the maid, and Carolena was furious at herself for being disappointed.

"*Signorina?* His Highness has asked me to accompany you to dinner. He's waiting on the terrace."

What about Abby and Vincenzo? "Thank you for coming to get me."

No shortcuts through the grounds this time, but it gave Carolena the opportunity to see more of the ornate palace. By the time she arrived at the terrace, Vincenzo had already joined the prince, but there was no sign of Abby or Max. The two men stood together chatting quietly.

She had the impression this terrace was a recent addition. It was a masterpiece of black-and-white marble checkerboard flooring, Moorish elements and cream-colored lattice furniture in Italian provincial. A collection of exotic trees and flowering plants gave the impression they were in a garden.

Valentino's dark blue gaze saw her first. He broke from Vincenzo and moved toward her wearing jeans and a sand-colored polo shirt. "*Buonasera,* Carolena. You look beautiful."

Don't say that. "Thank you."

His quick smile was a killer. "I hope you're hungry. I told the kitchen to prepare chicken the way Abby tells me you like it."

"You're very kind." Too kind. She flashed him a smile as he helped her get seated. Valentino had no equal as a host. She decided he had no equal, period.

Vincenzo walked over and kissed her cheek before sitting down at the round table opposite her. A sumptuous-looking meal had been laid out for them. A maid came out on the terrace just then and told Valentino his mother wanted to speak to him when he had a minute. He nodded before she left.

"Where's Abby, Vincenzo?"

"Max fussed all day and is still feverish, so we're taking turns."

"The poor little thing. Do you think it's serious?"

"We don't know. Our doctor said it could be a virus, but Max isn't holding down his food. That has me worried."

"I don't blame you. Is there something I can do to help?"

"Yes," Valentino inserted. "If Max is still sick tomorrow, you can keep me company, since Vincenzo will be tied up taking care of his family."

He actually sounded happy about it, but the news filled Carolena with consternation. She'd been with him too much already and her attraction to him was growing. She flicked him a glance. "You don't have to worry about entertaining me. I brought my laptop and always have work to do."

"Not while you're here." Valentino's underlying tone of authority quieted any more of her excuses. "No doubt you and Abby had intended to visit some of the shops and museums in Gemelli while on holiday, but I can think of something more exciting for tomorrow *if* you're up to it."

Vincenzo shot her a glance she couldn't decipher. "Be careful."

She chuckled. "Is that a warning?"

After finishing his coffee, a glimmer of a smile appeared. "On my first business visit here years ago, Valentino dangled the same option in front of me."

"What happened?"

He studied her for a moment. "That's for you to find out."

"Now you've made me nervous."

"Maybe you should be." She couldn't tell if Vincenzo's cryptic response was made in jest or not.

"You've frightened her," Valentino muttered. Again, Carolena was confused by the more serious undertone of their conversation.

"Then I'm sorry and I apologize." Vincenzo put down his napkin and got to his feet. "Enjoy your evening. We'll talk again in the morning. Please don't get up."

"Kiss that baby for me and give Abby my love."

"I will."

She'd never seen Vincenzo so preoccupied. Being a new father wasn't easy, but she sensed something else was on his mind, as well.

"What went on just now?" she asked as soon as he left the terrace.

Valentino had been watching her through narrowed eyes. "I'm afraid he thinks my idea of a good time could backfire." Carolena believed there was more to it than that, but she let it go for now.

"You mean it might be one of those surprises that's the wrong kind for me?"

"Possibly."

"Well, if you don't tell me pretty soon, I might expire on the spot from curiosity."

She thought he'd laugh, but for once he didn't. "I'd like to take you sailing to Taormina. It's an island Goethe called 'a part of paradise.' The medieval streets have tiny passages with secrets I can guarantee you'll love."

"It sounds wonderful, but that wasn't the place you had in mind when you were talking with Vincenzo."

"I've had time to think the better of it."

A rare flare of temper brought blood to her cheeks. "Vincenzo is Abby's husband, not mine."

"And he enjoys her confidence."

"In other words, he's trying to protect me from something he thinks wouldn't be good for me."

"Maybe."

Carolena's grandmother used to try to protect her the same way. But if she got into it with the prince, she'd be acting like the willful child her grandparent used to accuse her of being. Averting her eyes, she forced herself to calm down and said, "It's possible Max will be better, but in case he isn't, I'd love a chance to go sailing. It's very kind of you."

She heard his sharp intake of breath. "Now you're patronizing me."

"What do you expect me to do? Have a tantrum?" The question was out of her mouth before she could stop it. She was mortified to realize she was out of control. Something had gotten into her. She didn't feel at all herself.

"At least it would be better than your pretense to mollify me," came the benign response.

What? "If you weren't the prince—"

"I asked you to forget my title."

"That's kind of hard to do."

"Why don't you finish what you were about to say. If I weren't the prince…"

"Bene." She sucked in her breath. "If neither of you were princes, I'd tell you I've been taking care of myself for twenty-seven years and don't need a couple of guys I hardly know to decide what's best for me. If that sounds ungracious, I didn't mean for it to offend you, but you did ask."

A look of satisfaction entered his eyes. "I was hoping you would say that. How would you like to fly up on Etna with me in a helicopter? We'll put down in one spot and I'll show you some sights no visitor gets to see otherwise."

Gulp. She clung to the edge of the table from sheer unadulterated excitement. Valentino intended to show her that ten-thousand-foot volcano up close? After seeing that movie, what person in the world wouldn't want the opportunity? She couldn't understand why Vincenzo thought it might not be a good experience for her.

"You love your work so much you'd go up there on your day off?"

"You can ask that after what I revealed to you today? Didn't you tell me you thought it sounded thrilling?"

"Yes." She stood up and gazed into those intelligent,

dark blue eyes. Ignoring the warning flags telling her to
be prudent, she said, "I'd absolutely love it."

A stillness surrounded them. "Never let it be said I
didn't give you an out."

"I don't want one, even if Vincenzo thought I did."

A tiny nerve throbbed at the side of his hard jaw.
"If Max is still sick in the morning, we'll leave around
eight-thirty. You'll need to wear jeans and a T-shirt if
you brought one. If not, you can wear one of mine."

"I have one."

"Good, but you can't go in sandals."

"I brought my walking boots."

"Perfect."

"I'll see you in the morning then."

As she started to leave, he said, "Don't go yet."

*Valentino—I can't spend any more time with you to-
night. I just can't!* "Your mother is waiting for you and
I have things to do. I know the way back to my room."

"Carolena?"

With a pounding heart, she paused at the entrance.
"Yes?"

"I enjoyed today more than you know."

Oh, but I do, her heart cried.

"The horseback ride was wonderful. Thank you
again." In the next breath she took off for the other
wing of the palace. Her efforts to stay away from him
weren't working. To see where he spent his time and
share it with him was too great a temptation to turn
down, but she recognized that the thing she'd prayed
would never happen was happening!

She was starting to care about him, way too much.

Forget the guilt over Berto's death that had prevented
her from getting close to another man. Her feelings were
way too strong for Valentino. Already she was terrified
at the thought of handling another loss when she had to
fly back to Arancia with Abby and Vincenzo.

But if she said she wasn't feeling well now and
begged off going with him tomorrow, he'd never believe her. Though she knew she was walking into emo-
tional danger by getting more involved, she didn't have
the strength to say no to him. *Help.*

CHAPTER THREE

LETTING CAROLENA GO when it was the last thing he wanted, Valentino walked through the palace to his mother's suite. The second he entered her sitting room he was met with the news he'd been dreading all his adult life.

While he'd been riding horses with Carolena, his mother had worked out the details of his coming marriage to Princess Alexandra of Cyprus. Both royal families had wanted a June wedding, but he'd asked for more time, hoping for another year of freedom. Unfortunately they'd forced him to settle on August tenth and now there was no possibility of him changing his mind.

Tonight his mother had pinned him down, gaining his promise there'd be no more women. By giving his word, it was as good as writing it in cement.

Ages ago he and Michelina had talked about their arranged marriages. Valentino had intended to be true to Alexandra once their marriage date was set, but he'd told Michelina he planned to live a full life with other women until his time came.

She, on the other hand, never did have the same problem because she'd fallen in love with Vincenzo long before they were married and would never have been unfaithful to him. Vincenzo was a good man who'd kept his marriage vows despite the fact that he didn't feel the same way about her. Valentino admired him more than any man he knew for being the best husband he could under the circumstances.

But after seeing Abby and Vincenzo together while they'd been here, he longed for that kind of love. A huge change had come over Vincenzo once he and Abby had fallen for each other. He was no longer the same man. Valentino could see the passion that leaped between them. Last night he'd witnessed it and knew such a deep envy, he could hardly bear it.

After eight months of marriage their love had grown stronger and deeper. Everyone could see it, his mother most of all. Both she and Valentino had suffered for Michelina. She'd had the misfortune of loving Vincenzo who couldn't love her back in the same way. It would have been better if she hadn't fallen for him, but he couldn't handle thinking about that right now.

The only thing to do where Alexandra was concerned was try to get pregnant soon and build a family the way his own parents had done. Even if the most important element was missing, children would fill a big hole. That's what Michelina had tried to do by going ahead with the surrogacy procedure.

Unfortunately, he hadn't counted on the existence of Carolena Baretti. Her unexpected arrival in Gemelli had knocked him sideways for reasons he hadn't been able to identify yet. Instead of imagining his future life, his thoughts kept running to the gorgeous brunette who was a guest in the other wing of the palace.

Something had happened to him since he'd come upon Abby's friend in the swimming pool that first evening. He'd promised his mother no more women and he'd meant it. But like a lodestone he'd once found on an ancient volcano crater attracting his tools, her unique personality and stunning physical traits had drawn him in.

He'd met many beautiful women in his life, but never one like her. For one thing, she hadn't thrown herself at him. Quite the opposite. That in itself was so rare he found himself attracted on several levels.

Because she was Abby's best friend, she was already in the untouchable category, even if he hadn't promised his mother. Yet this evening, the last thing he'd wanted to do was say good-night to her.

They'd shared a lot today. Intimate things. Her concern for him, the tears she'd shed for his uncle, touched him on a profound level. He'd never met a woman so completely genuine. To his chagrin she made him feel close to her. To his further disgust, he couldn't think beyond having breakfast with her in the morning.

With his blood effectively chilled now that the conversation with his mother was over, he excused himself and called for his car to come around to his private entrance. He told his driver to head for Tancredi's Restaurant on the east end of the island, a twenty-minute drive.

Once on his way, he phoned his best friend from his university days to alert him he was coming. Matteo owned the place since his father had died. He would be partying in the bar with a few of their mutual friends now that there were no more customers.

After the limo turned down the alley behind the restaurant, Matteo emerged from the backdoor and climbed inside.

"Ehi, Valentino—"

"Sorry I'm late, but tonight certain things were unavoidable."

"Non c'è problema! It's still early for us. Come on. We've been waiting for you."

"I'm afraid I can't."

"Ooh. Adriana's not going to like hearing that."

"She's the reason I asked you to come out to the limo. Can I depend on you to put it to her gently that I won't be seeing her again?"

He frowned. "Why not?"

They stared at each other before Matteo let out an epithet. "Does this mean you're finally getting married?" He knew the union had been arranged years ago.

Valentino grimaced. "Afraid so." Once he'd gone to his mother's apartment, she'd forced him to come to a final decision after talking with his betrothed's parents. "They're insisting on an August wedding and coronation. The president of the parliament will announce our formal engagement next week."

He realized it was long past time to end his brief, shallow relationship with Adriana. For her best interest he should have done it a month ago. Instinct told him she would be a willing mistress after his marriage, but Valentino didn't feel that way about her or any woman. In any case, he would never go down that path.

Matteo's features hardened. "I can't believe this day has finally come. It's like a bad dream."

A groan escaped Valentino's throat. "But one I'm committed to. I've told you before, but I'll say it again. You've been a great friend, Matteo. I'll never forget."

"Are you saying goodbye to me, too?" he asked quietly.

His friend's question hurt him. "How can you even ask me that?"

"I don't know." Matteo drove his fist into his other palm. "I knew one day there was going to be a wedding and coronation and I know of your loyalty. Now everything's going to change."

"Not my friendship with you."

"I hope not. It's meant everything to me."

"My father told me a king has no friends, but I'm not the king yet. Even when I am, you'll always be my friend. I'll call you soon." He clapped him on the shoulder before Matteo got out of the limo. Once he'd disappeared inside the restaurant, Valentino told his driver to head back to the palace. But his mood was black.

After a sleepless night he learned that Max wasn't any better, so he followed through on his plans to pick up Carolena at her apartment. He found her outside her door waiting for him. The sight of her in jeans and a T-shirt caused another adrenaline rush.

Her eyes lifted to his. "Is there anything else you can think of I might need before we leave?"

He'd already taken inventory of her gorgeous figure and still hadn't recovered. "We'll be flying to the center in my helicopter. Whatever is missing we will find there."

"Then I'm ready." Carolena shut the suite and followed him down the hallway and out the doors. They crossed the grounds to the pad where his helicopter was waiting. "I hope this isn't a dream and I'm going to wake up in a few minutes. To see where you spend your time kept me awake all night."

Nothing could have pleased Valentino more than to know she was an adventurous woman who'd taken an interest in his research. But he knew in his gut her interest in him went deeper than that. "Perhaps now you'll understand that after a day's work on the volcano, I have trouble getting to sleep, too."

Besides his family and bodyguards, plus close friends like Matteo, he rarely shared his love for his work with anyone outside of his colleagues at the center. For his own protection, the women he'd had relationships with knew nothing about his life.

He'd called ahead to one of the center's pilots who would be taking them up. The helicopter was waiting for them when they touched down.

"Dante Serrano, meet Signorina Carolena Baretti from Arancia. She's the best friend of my brother-in-law's wife. They're staying at the palace with me for a few days. I thought she might like to see Etna at closer range."

The pilot's eyes flared in male admiration and surprise before he shook Carolena's hand and welcomed her aboard. This was a first for Valentino, let alone for Dante, who'd never known Valentino to fly a female with him unless she happened to be a geologist doing work.

He helped her into the seat behind the pilot, then took the copilot's seat. While the rotors whined, he turned to her. "Your first volcano experience should be from the air."

"I'm so excited to be seeing this up close, I can hardly stand it." Her enthusiasm was contagious. "Why does it constantly smoke?"

"That's because it's continually being reshaped by seismic activity. There are four distinct craters at the summit and more than three hundred vents on the flanks. Some are small holes, others are large craters. You'll see things that are invisible or look completely different from the surface."

"You're so right!" she cried after they took off. Once they left Catania, they passed over the fertile hillsides and lush pines. "The vistas are breathtaking, Val. With the Mediterranean for a background, these snow-topped mountains are fabulous. I didn't expect to see so much green and blue."

Her reaction, on top of her beautiful face, made it impossible for Valentino to look anywhere else. "It's a universe all its own."

'I can't believe what I'm seeing."

The landscape changed as they flew higher and higher. "We're coming up on some black lava deserts. Take a good look. Mount Etna is spitting lava more violently than it has in years, baffling us. Not only is it unpredictable, the volcano is raging, erupting in rapid succession."

He loved her awestruck squeals of delight. "I suppose you've walked across those deserts."

"I've climbed all over this volcano with Uncle Stefano."

"No wonder you love your work so much! I would, too!"

"The range of ash fall is much wider than usual. That's why I always come home dirty."

"Now I understand. Come to think of it, you did look like you'd been putting out a fire."

Dante shared a grin with Valentino. "Signorina Baretti," He spoke over his shoulder. "Even in ancient times, the locals marveled at the forces capable of shooting fountains of lava into the sky. In Greek and Roman mythology, the volcano is represented by a limping blacksmith swinging his hammer as sparks fly.

"Legend has it that the natural philosopher Empedocles jumped into the crater two thousand five hundred years ago. What he found there remained his secret because he never returned. All that remained of him were his iron shoes, which the mountain later spat out."

"That's a wonderful story, if not frightening."

All three of them laughed.

"The really fascinating part is coming up. We're headed for the Bove Valley, Etna's huge caldera. You're going to get a bird's-eye view of the eastern slope." They flew on with Dante giving her the full treatment of the famous volcano that produced more stunned cries from Carolena.

"How big is it?"

"Seven kilometers from east to west, six kilometers from north to south."

She was glued to the window, mesmerized. Valentino knew how she felt. He signaled Dante to fly them to Bocca Nuova.

"When we set down on the side of the pit, you'll see a new fumarole in the saddle between the old and new southeast crater. I want you to stay by me. This is where I was working the other day. You won't need a gas mask at this distance, but you can understand why I want every citizen of Gemelli to be equipped with one."

"After seeing this and hearing about your uncle Stefano, I understand your concern, believe me."

Before long, he helped her out and they walked fifty yards to a vantage point. "This is a place no one is allowed except our teams. The organized tours of the thousands of people who came to Etna are much farther below."

Soon they saw the vent releasing the same bluish gas and ash he'd recorded the other day.

"This fumarole was formed by that long fissure you can see."

While they stood there gazing, the noise of explosions coming from deep within the volcano shook the ground. When she cried out, he automatically put his arm around her shoulders and pulled her tight against his side. He liked the feel of her womanly body this close.

"Don't be alarmed," he murmured into her fragrant hair. "We're safe or I wouldn't have brought you up here."

She clung to him. "I know that, but I have to tell you a secret. I never felt insignificant until now." Those were his very thoughts the first time he'd come up on Etna. After a long silence, she lifted her eyes to him. In them he saw a longing for him that she couldn't hide when she said, "It's awesome and mind blowing all at the same time."

Those dazzling, dark-fringed green eyes blew him away, but not for the reasons she'd been alluding to. He was terrified over the feelings he'd developed for her. "You've taken the words right out of my mouth."

The desire to kiss her was so powerful, it took all the self-control he possessed not to crush her against him. He was in serious trouble and knew it.

Fighting his desire, he said, "I think you've seen enough for today. We've been gone a long time and need to eat. Another day and I'll take you on a hike through some lava fields and tunnels you'll find captivating." *Almost as captivating as I'm finding you.*

"I doubt I'll ever be in Gemelli again, but if I am, I'll certainly take you up on your offer. Thank you for a day I'll never *ever* forget." He felt her tremulous voice shake his insides.

"Nor will I." The fact that she was off-limits had no meaning to him right now.

On their way back to the center, he checked his phone messages. One from Vincenzo and two from his mother. He checked Vincenzo's first.

I'm just giving you a heads-up. Max isn't doing well, so we're flying back to Arancia at nine in the morning. Sorry about this, but the doctor thinks he may have gas-

troenteritis and wants to check him out at the hospital.
Give me a call when you're available.

Valentino's lips thinned. He was sorry about the baby, but it meant Carolena would be leaving in the morning.

The queen's first message told him she was upset they were going to have to leave with her grandson. She was crazy about Max and her reaction was understandable. Her second message had to do with wedding preparations. Since he couldn't do anything about either situation at the moment, he decided to concentrate on Carolena, who would be slipping away from his life much sooner than he'd anticipated.

Once they touched down at the center and had thanked Dante for the wonderful trip, they climbed on board Valentino's helicopter. But instead of flying back to the palace where his mother expected him to join her the second he got back, he instructed his pilot to land on the royal yacht anchored in the bay. They could have dinner on board away from the public eye.

Carolena was a very special VIP and the crew would think nothing of his entertaining the close friend of his new sister-in-law who was here with the prince of Arancia visiting the queen.

He called ahead to arrange for their meal to be served on deck. After they arrived on board and freshened up, they sat down to dinner accompanied by soft rock music as the sun disappeared below the horizon. Both of them had developed an appetite. Valentino loved it that she ate with enjoyment.

"Try the Insolia wine. It has a slightly nutty flavor

with a finish that is a combination of sweet fruit and sour citrus. I think it goes well with swordfish."

"It definitely does, and the steak is out of this world, Val. Everything here in Gemelli is out of this world."

From the deck they could see Etna smoking in the far distance. She kept looking at it. "To think I flew over that volcano today and saw a fumarole up close." Her gaze swerved to his. "Nothing I'll ever do in life will match the wonder of this day, and it's all because of you."

He sipped his wine. "So the surprise didn't turn out to be so bad, after all."

"You know it didn't." Her voice throbbed, revealing her emotion. "I can't think why Vincenzo warned me against it. Unless—"

When she didn't finish, he said, "Unless what?"

"Maybe watching Michelina when she had her riding accident has made him more cautious than usual over the people he loves and cares about. Last night I could tell how worried he was about Max."

Valentino hadn't thought of that, but he couldn't rule it out as a possibility, though he didn't think it was Vincenzo's major concern. Now that they were talking about it, his conversation at dinner with Vincenzo in front of her came back to haunt him.

He'd been warning Valentino, but maybe not about the volcano. Unfortunately, Vincenzo had always been a quick study. Possibly he'd picked up on Valentino's interest in Carolena. Whatever had gone on in Vincenzo's mind, now was the time to tell her about the change in their plans to fly back to Arancia.

"I checked my voice mail on the way to the yacht. You can listen." He pulled his cell phone from his pocket and let her hear Vincenzo's message.

In an instant everything changed, as he knew it would. "The poor darling. It's a good thing we're going home in the morning. I'm sure Max will be all right, but after no sleep, all three of them have to be absolutely miserable."

Make that an even four.

The idea of Carolena leaving Gemelli filled him with a sense of loss he'd never experienced before. The deaths of his father and sister were different. It didn't matter that he'd only known her twenty-four hours. To never be with her again was anathema to him.

He could have predicted what she'd say next. "We'd better get back to the palace. I need to pack."

"Let's have our dessert first. You have to try *cassata alla sicilana.*" Anything to prolong their time together.

"Isn't that a form of cheesecake?"

"Cake like you've never tasted anywhere else."

An impish smile broke one corner of her voluptuous mouth. "Something tells me you're a man who loves his sweets."

"Why do you think that?"

"I don't know. Maybe it's because of the way you embrace life to the fullest and enjoy its richness while at the same time reverencing it. When the gods handed out gifts, you received more than your fair share."

He frowned. "What do you mean?"

"There aren't many men who could measure up to

you. Your sister used to sing your praises to Abby, who said she worshipped you."

"The feeling was mutual, believe me."

"According to Abby, Michelina admitted that the only man who came close to you was Prince Vincenzo. That's high praise indeed. Luckily for your country, you're going to be in charge one day."

One day? That day was almost upon him!

For the wedding date to have been fixed at the same time he'd met Signorina Baretti, the pit in Valentino's stomach had already grown into a caldera bigger than the one he'd shown her today.

He'd spun out every bit of time with her he could squeeze and had no legitimate choice but to take her back to the palace.

"It's getting late. I'm sure Vincenzo will want to talk to you tonight."

Valentino shook his head. "With the baby sick, that won't be happening." In truth, he wasn't up to conversation with Vincenzo or his mother. For the first time in his life he had the wicked instinct to do what he wanted and kidnap this woman who'd beguiled him.

"I have a better idea. It's been a long day. We'll stay on the yacht and fly you back on time in the morning. I'll instruct the maid to pack your things. As for tonight, anything you need we have on board."

Carolena's breath caught. "What about your girlfriend? Won't she be expecting you?"

His dark blue eyes narrowed on her face. "Not when I'm entertaining family and friends. As for the other question you don't dare ask, I've never brought a woman on board the yacht or taken one up on the volcano."

He'd been so frank and honest with her today, she believed him now. His admission shook her to her core. "If I didn't know better, I would think you were propositioning me," she teased to cover her chaotic emotions. There she went again. Saying something she shouldn't have allowed to escape her lips.

His jaw hardened. "I'm a man before being a prince and I *am* propositioning you, but I can see I've shocked you as much as myself."

She could swear that was truth she'd heard come out of him. Carolena was Abby's friend, yet that hadn't stopped him, and obviously that fact wasn't stopping her. It was as if they were both caught in a snare of such intense attraction, they knew no boundaries.

"Do you want to know something else?" he murmured. "I can see in those glorious green eyes of yours that you'd like to stay on board with me tonight. True desire is something you can't hide. We've both felt it since we met, so there's no use denying it."

"I'm not," she confessed in a tremulous voice. Carolena could feel her defenses crumbling and started to tremble. Never had she been around a man who'd made her feel so completely alive.

"My kingdom for an honest woman, and here you are."

"Only you and Vincenzo could say such a thing and get away with it."

Her humor didn't seem to touch him. "Tell me about

the man who died. You *were* speaking about a man. Are you still terribly in love with him?"

His question reached the core of her being. "I'll always love him," she answered honestly.

He reached across the table and grasped her hand. "How long has he been gone?"

She couldn't lie to him. "Seven years."

After a moment of quiet, he said, "That's a long time to be in love with a memory. How did he die?"

"It doesn't matter. I don't want to talk about it."

Those all-seeing eyes of his gazed through to her soul. "Yet somehow you still feel responsible for his death?"

"Yes."

"Has it prevented you from getting close to another man?"

"I've been with other men since he died, if that's what you mean."

"Carolena—tell me the truth. Is there one man who's vitally important to you now?"

Yes. But he's not in Arancia.

"No one man more than another," she dissembled.

She heard his sharp intake of breath. "Then do you dare stay with me the way you dared to get close to Etna's furnace today? I'm curious to see how brave a woman you really are."

His thumb massaged her palm, sending warmth through her sensitized body until her toes curled. "You already know the answer to that."

"Dance with me, *bellissima*," he begged in a husky

whisper. "I don't give a damn that the crew can see us. You've entranced me and I need to feel you in my arms."

It was what she wanted, too. When she'd heard Vincenzo say that they were leaving in the morning, she'd wanted to cry out in protest that she'd only gotten here. She hadn't had enough time with Valentino. *Not nearly enough.*

He got up from the table and drew her into his arms. She went into them eagerly, aching for this since the time he'd put his arm around her up on the volcano. It felt as if their bodies were meant for each other. She slid her arms around his neck until there was no air between them. They clung out of need in the balmy night air that enveloped them like velvet.

His hands roved over her back and hips as they got a new sense of each other only touch could satisfy. They slow danced until she lost track of time. To hold and be held by this amazing man was a kind of heaven.

She knew he was unattainable. Abby had told her he'd been betrothed to Princess Alexandra in his teens, just like Vincenzo's betrothal to Princess Michelina. One day Valentino would have to marry. He'd explained all that yesterday.

Carolena understood that. It didn't bother her since she shunned the idea of commitment that would lead to her own marriage. Marriage meant being responsible for another person's happiness. She couldn't handle that, but selfishly she did desire this one night with Valentino before she flew back to Arancia and never saw him again.

Tonight he'd made her thankful she'd been born a

woman. Knowing he wanted her as much as she wanted him brought indescribable joy. One night with him would have to be enough, except that he still hadn't kissed her yet and she was dying for it. When he suddenly stopped moving, she moaned in disappointment.

His hands squeezed her upper arms. "The steward will show you downstairs to your cabin," he whispered before pulling the phone from his pocket. "I'll join you shortly."

Carolena was so far gone she'd forgotten about the prying eyes of the crew, but Valentino was used to the whole world watching him and did what was necessary to keep gossip to a minimum. Without words she eased away from him and walked over to the table for her purse before following the steward across the deck to the stairs.

The luxury yacht was a marvel, but Carolena was too filled with desire for Valentino to notice much of anything. Once she reached the cabin and the steward left, she took a quick shower and slipped into one of the white toweling bathrobes hanging on a hook. The dressing room provided every cosmetic and convenience a man or woman could need.

She sat in front of the mirror and brushed her hair. *Entranced* was the right word. Though she knew she'd remain single all her life, she felt as if this was her wedding night while she waited for him to come. The second he entered the room he would hear the fierce pounding of her heart.

Soon she heard his rap on the door. "Come in," she called quietly. He walked in and shut the door behind him, still dressed in the clothes he'd worn during their trip.

Without saying anything, he reached for her hand and drew her over to the bed where he sat down and pulled her between his legs. His gaze glowed like hot blue embers. Everywhere it touched, she was set on fire. Her ears picked up the ragged sound of his breathing.

"You look like a bride."

But, of course, she wasn't a bride, and she sensed something was wrong. She could feel it. "Is that good or bad?"

He ran his hands up and down her arms beneath the loose sleeves of her robe as if even his fingers were hungry for her. "Carolena—" There was an unmistakable plea for understanding in his tone.

"Yes?" Whatever was coming, she knew she wasn't going to like it.

"I talked frankly with you yesterday about my personal life. But what you couldn't know was that last night after you went back to your room, I met with my mother." His chest rose and fell visibly. "While you and I were out riding, my wedding date to Princess Alexandra was finally set in stone. We're being married on August tenth, the day of my coronation."

Carolena stood stock-still while the news sank in. That was only two months from now...

"Though I made the promise to my mother that I'd be faithful to Alexandra from here on out, I really made it to myself and have already gotten word to my latest girlfriend that it's over for good."

She could hardly credit what she was hearing.

"But little did I know I was already being tested by none other than Abby's best friend."

A small cry escaped her throat. "I shouldn't have come, but Abby kept insisting." She shivered. "This is all my fault, Val."

"There you go again, taking on blame for something that's no one's fault. If we were to follow that line of thinking, shall I blame myself for inviting Vincenzo to come on this trip? Shall we blame him for bringing his wife and her best friend?"

His logic made Carolena feel like a fool. "Of course not."

"At least you admit that much. In my whole life I've never wanted a woman more than I've wanted you, since the moment we met at the swimming pool. But it's more than that now. Much more."

"I know. I feel it, too." But she remained dry eyed and smiled at him. "The gods are jealous of you. They're waiting for you to make a mistake. Didn't you know that?"

He squeezed her hands gently. "When I dared you to stay with me tonight, I crossed a line I swore I would never do."

"I believe you. But the fact is, it takes two, Val. I didn't know your wedding date had been set, of course. Yet even knowing you were betrothed, I crossed it, too, because I've never known desire like this before, either. I've never had an affair before."

"Carolena..."

He said her name with such longing, she couldn't stand it. "Let's not make this situation any more impossible. Go back to the palace tonight knowing you've passed your test."

"And leave you like this?" he cried urgently, pulling her closer to him. "You don't really mean that!"

"Yes. I do. You have Vincenzo to think about, and a mother who's waiting for your return. Your wedding's going to take place soon. You need to concentrate on Alexandra now."

But she knew he wasn't listening. He got to his feet, cupping her face in his hands. "I don't want to leave you." He sounded as if he was in agony. "Say the word and I won't."

Abby could hear her grandmother's voice. *You go where angels fear to tread without worrying about anyone else but yourself.*

Not this time, *nonnina.*

"Thank you for your honesty. It's one of your most sterling qualities. You truly are the honorable man your sister idolized. But I have enough sins on my conscience without helping you add one to yours."

His brows formed a bar above his eyes. "You told me you caused the death of the man you loved, but you also said it wasn't intentional."

She averted her eyes. "It wasn't."

"Then no sin has been committed."

"Not if we part now. I don't want you going through life despising yourself for breaking the rule you've set. Believe it or not, I *want* you to go, Val," she told him. "After the promise you made to your parents when your uncle died, I couldn't handle it otherwise."

"Handle what? You're still holding back on me. Tell me what it is."

"It's no longer of any importance."

"Carolena—"

He was willing to break his vow for her because he wanted her that much. Just knowing that helped her to stay strong. But he didn't realize all this had to do with her self-preservation.

"Val, if it's all right with you, I'd like to remain on board until tomorrow morning and then fly back to the palace. But please know that when I leave Gemelli, I'll take home the memory of a man who for a moment out of time made me feel immortal. I'll treasure the memory of you all my life."

She pulled away from him and walked over to the door to open it. *"Addio,* sweet prince."

CHAPTER FOUR

THE MOMENT VALENTINO walked into the palace at eleven that night, he texted Vincenzo, who was still up. They met in Valentino's suite.

"How did your day go?" his brother-in-law asked after he'd walked into the sitting room.

Valentino was still on fire for the woman who'd looked like a vision when he'd walked into her cabin.

"After we left Etna, I thought Carolena would like dinner on the yacht where there's a wonderful view of the island. She's staying there overnight. My pilot will fly her back in the morning. You should have seen her when we got out of the helicopter and walked over to view one of the fumaroles. She was one person who really appreciated the experience."

"Michelina would never step foot on Etna and was always afraid for you. Sorry about this morning. I guess I thought it might frighten Carolena."

Valentino had forgotten about his sister's fear. It showed how totally concentrated he'd been on Carolena. "If she was, she hid it well. Now I want to hear about Max. How is he?"

"For the moment both he and Abby are asleep. It'll be a relief to get him home. After the doctor tells us what's wrong and we can relax, I'd like it if you could arrange to fly to Arancia so we can talk business."

He nodded. "I'm as anxious as you to get started on the idea we've discussed. I'll clear my calendar." It would mean seeing Carolena again. He was going to get the truth out of her one way or another.

"Abby thinks Carolena would be a good person to consult over the legalities of the plans we have in mind. Did I mention her expertise is patent law? It's exactly what we need."

She was a patent attorney? Valentino's heart leaped to think he didn't need to find an excuse to see her again when he had a legitimate reason to be with her before long. On his way to the palace, he'd come close to telling the pilot he'd changed his mind and wanted to go back to the yacht.

"Valentino? Did you hear what I said?"

"Sorry. The news about her work in patent law took me by surprise. Abby and Carolena are both intelligent women. With them being such close friends and attorneys, it will be a pleasure to have them consult with us. I've worried about finding someone we could really trust."

"Amen to that. We don't want anyone else to get wind of this until it's a fait accompli," Vincenzo muttered. "Abby asked me to thank you for taking such good care of Carolena today."

If he only knew how dangerously close Valentino had come to making love to her. Once that happened, there'd be no going back because he knew in his gut he'd want her over and over again. That would jeopardize both their lives and put them in a different kind of hell.

"It's always a rush to go up on Etna with someone who finds it as fascinating as I do."

"She really liked it?"

"I wish I had a recording while we were in the air."

Vincenzo smiled. "That'll make Abby happy. She brought Carolena along because seven years ago yesterday her fiancé was killed days before she became a bride. Apparently this date in June is always hard for her. They were very much in love."

Fiancé?

Valentino's gut twisted in deepest turmoil when he remembered telling her she looked like a bride. More than ever he was determined to find out what kind of guilt she'd been carrying around all this time.

"Abby says she dates one man after another, but it's only once or twice, never really getting to know anyone well. She believes she's depressed and is pretty worried about her. Abby was hoping this trip would help her get out of herself. Sounds like your day on the volcano may have done just that."

The revelations coming one after the other hit Valentino like a volcanic bomb during an eruption.

"I hope so."

"I'd better get back to our suite. It'll be my turn to walk the floor with Max when he wakes up again. My poor wife is worn out."

"From the looks of it, so are you." He patted Vincenzo on the shoulder before walking him to the door.

"I'll have breakfast sent to your suite at eight. Carolena will be waiting for you on the helicopter."

"Thanks for everything, Valentino."

"The queen says this will pass. She ought to know after raising me and my siblings. See you in the morning."

After his brother-in-law left, Valentino raced out of the palace to the swimming pool. He did laps until he was so exhausted he figured he might be able to sleep for what was left of the rest of the night. But that turned out to be a joke. There were certain fires you couldn't put out.

The next morning when he walked out to the landing pad with Vincenzo and his family, Carolena was still strapped in her seat. One of his security men put the luggage from her room on board as he climbed in.

Other than a smile and another thank-you for the tour of the volcano, she displayed no evidence of having missed Valentino or passing a tormented night. They were both accomplished actors playing roles with such expertise they might even have deceived each other. Except for the slight break he heard in her voice that caused his heart to skip several beats.

Four days later Carolena had just finished taking a deposition in her office and had said goodbye to her client when her new secretary, Tomaso, told her Abby was on the line. She hoped it was good news about the baby and picked up.

"Abby? How are you? How's Max?"

"He's doing great. The gastroenteritis is finally gone."

"Thank heaven!"

"I feel so terrible about what happened on our trip."

"Why do you say that? I was sorry for you, of course, but I had a wonderful time!"

"You're always such a good sport. I know it made Valentino's day for someone to be excited about his work."

"He's an incredible man, Abby." Carolena tried to keep the tremor out of her voice.

"He was impressed with you, too. That's one of the reasons I'm calling. He flew into Arancia this morning so he and Vincenzo can talk business."

She almost had heart failure. It was a good thing she was sitting down. Valentino was here?

"Since you're a patent law attorney, both men want you to meet with them. They need your legal counsel along with mine."

Her pulse raced off the chart. "Why?" She'd thought she'd never see him again and had been in such a depression, she'd decided that if she didn't get over it, she would have to go for professional help.

"They're putting together a monumental idea to benefit both our countries. I'll tell you all about it when you get here. Can you come to the palace after work? The four of us will talk and have dinner together."

Carolena jumped up from her leather chair. No, no, no. She didn't dare put herself into a position like that again. Legitimate or not, Valentino had to know how hard this was going to be for her. She didn't have his self-control.

If for any reason she happened to end up alone with him tonight, she might beg him to let her spend the night because she couldn't help herself. How wicked would that be? She'd spend the rest of her life mourning another loss because there could never be another time with him. This was one time Carolena couldn't do what Abby was asking.

"I'm afraid I can't."

"Why not?"

"I have a date for the symphony."

"Then cancel it. I just found out this morning that Valentino is rushed for time. Did I tell you his wedding and coronation are coming up in August?"

She bit her lip. "No. I don't believe you mentioned it."

"He'd hoped to get this business settled before flying back to Gemelli tomorrow."

Here today, gone tomorrow? She couldn't bear it. This request had put her in an untenable position. What to do so she wouldn't offend her friend? After racking her brain, she came up with one solution that might work. It would *have* to work since Carolena didn't dare make a wrong move now.

She gripped the phone tighter. "I have an idea that won't waste Valentino's time. Would it be possible if you three came to the office this afternoon?" Neutral ground rather than the palace was the only way for her to stay out of temptation's way.

"I'm afraid not. It would require too much security for the two of them to meet anywhere else. The security risk is higher than usual with Valentino's coronation coming up soon. How would it be if you cleared your slate for this afternoon and came to the palace? Say two o'clock?"

By now Carolena was trembling.

"We'll talk and eat out by the pool. If you leave the palace by six-thirty, you'll be in time for your date."

Carolena panicked. "I'd have to juggle some appointments." That was another lie. "I don't know if Signor Faustino will let me. I'm working on a big case."

"Bigger than the one for the princes of two countries?" Abby teased.

Her friend had put her on the royal spot. The writing was on the wall. "I—I'll arrange it." Her voice faltered.

"Perfect. The limo will pick you up at the office at one forty-five. Come right out to the terrace by the pool after you arrive."

"All right," she whispered before hanging up.

In an hour and a half Carolena would be seeing Valentino again. Already she had this suffocating feeling in her chest. It was a good thing she had another client to take up her time before the limo came for her. When she left the office she'd tell Tomaso she was going out for a business lunch with a client, which was only the truth.

Luckily she'd worn her sleeveless black designer shift dress with the crew neck and black belt to work. She'd matched the outfit with black heels. There was no need to do anything about her hair. All she had to do was touch up her makeup. When she showed up at the palace, it would carry out the lie that she'd be going to the symphony later.

Valentino had just finished some laps in the pool when he saw Carolena walk past the garden toward them in a stunning, formfitting black dress. Only a woman with her figure could wear it. Abby had told him she was going to the symphony later with a man.

She'd parted her hair in the middle above her forehead and had swept a small braid from each side around to the back, leaving her dark hair long. Two-tiered silvery earrings dangled between the strands. He did a somersault off the wall of the pool to smother his gasp.

If he'd hoped that she wouldn't look as good to him after four days, he could forget that! The trick would be to keep his eyes off her while they tried to do business. While Abby laid out their lunch beneath the overhang, Vincenzo sat at one of the tables working on his laptop. Both of them wore beach robes over their swimsuits. Max was down for a nap in the nursery.

She headed for Abby. A low whistle came out of Vincenzo and he got up to greet her. "I've never seen you looking lovelier, Carolena."

"Thank you," she said as the two women hugged.

Valentino climbed out of the shallow end of the pool and threw on a beach cover-up. "We're grateful you could come this afternoon."

Carolena shot him a brief glance. "It's very nice to see you again, Val. Signor Faustino was thrilled when he found out where I was going. Needless to say, he considers it the coup of the century that I've been summoned to help the princes of Gemelli and Arancia with a legal problem."

Abby was all smiles. "Knowing him, he'll probably make you senior partner at their next meeting."

"Don't wish that on me!" That sounded final.

Valentino moved closer. "You mean, it isn't your dream?"

"Definitely not." She seemed so composed, but it was deceiving, because he saw a nerve throbbing frantically at the base of her throat where he longed to kiss her.

He smiled. "Our conversation on the deck of the yacht was cut short and didn't give us time to cover your dreams before I had to leave."

Being out of the sun, she couldn't blame it for the rose blush that crept into her face. "As I recall, we were discussing *your* dreams for Gemelli, Val."

Touché. But his unrealized personal dream that had lain dormant deep in his soul since his cognizance of life was another matter altogether.

"In truth, I hope to make enough money from the law practice that one day in the future I can buy back my grandparents' small farm and work it." Her green eyes clouded for a moment. "I'm a farmer's daughter at heart."

"I understand your parents are not alive."

"No, nor are my grandparents. Their farm was sold. There have been Barettis in Arancia for almost a hundred years. I'm the only Baretti left and want to keep up the tradition by buying the place back."

Had her fiancé been a farmer, too? Valentino knew a moment of jealousy that she'd loved someone else enough to create such a powerful emotion in her.

"I had no idea," he murmured, "but since it's in your blood, that makes you doubly valuable for the task at hand." His mind was teeming with new ideas to keep her close to him.

"Abby said you and Vincenzo were planning some-thing monumental for both your countries. I confess I'm intrigued."

"Hey, you two," Abby called to them. "Come and help yourselves to lunch first, then we'll get down to business."

He followed Carolena to the serving table. After they'd filled their plates, they sat down at one of the round tables where the maid poured them iced tea. Once they'd started eating, he said, "Vincenzo? Why don't you lay the groundwork for the women and we'll go from there."

"Our two countries have a growing problem be-cause of the way they are situated on coastal waters. We all know the land around the Mediterranean is one of the most coveted terrains on earth. Over the years, our prime properties of orange and lemon groves that have sustained our economies for centuries have been shrinking due to man's progress. Our farmers are being inundated with huge sums of money to sell their land so it can be developed for commercial tourism."

"I know that's true," Carolena commented. "My grandfather was approached many times to sell, but he wouldn't do it."

Vincenzo nodded. "He's the type of traditional farmer fighting a battle to hold on to his heritage. Farm-ers are losing their workers, who want to go to the city. In the process, we're losing a vital and precious resource that has caused Valentino and me to lose sleep. Some-thing has to be done to stop the trend and rebuild the greatness of what we've always stood for. We've come up with an idea to help our farmers by giving them a new incentive. You tell them, Valentino."

Carolena's gaze swerved to him. He could tell Vincenzo had grabbed the women's attention.

"We need to compete with other countries to increase our exports to fill the needs of a growing world market and build our economies here at home. The lemons of Arancia are highly valued because of their low acidity and delicate flavor.

"Likewise the blood oranges of Gemelli are sought after for their red flesh and deep red juice. The juice is exceptionally healthy, being rich in antioxidants. What we're proposing is to patent our fruit in a joint venture so we can grow an enviable exporting business.

"With a unique logo and marketing strategy, we can put our citrus fruits front and center in the world market. When the buyer sees it, they'll know they're getting authentic fruit from our regions alone and clamor for it."

"That's a wonderful idea," Carolena exclaimed. "You would need to be filed as a Consortium for the Promotion of the Arancian Lemon and the Gemellian Blood Orange. The IGP logo will be the official acknowledgment that the lemons and oranges were grown in your territories according to the traditional rules."

Vincenzo leaned forward. "That's exactly what we're striving for. With the right marketing techniques, the citrus business should start to flourish again. We'll come up with a name for the logo."

"That's easy," Abby volunteered. "AG. Two tiny letters stamped on each fruit. You'll have to make a video that could be distributed to every country where you want to introduce your brand."

Bless you, Abby. She was reading Valentino's mind. He needed more time alone with Carolena to talk about their lives. Abby had just given him the perfect excuse. He exchanged glances with Vincenzo before he looked at Carolena.

"The right video would sell the idea quickly, but we need a spokesperson doing the video to put it across. You'd be the perfect person for several reasons, Carolena."

"Oh, no." He saw the fear in her eyes and knew exactly what put it there, but he couldn't help himself. What he felt for Carolena was stronger than anything he'd ever known.

"You have the looks and education to sell our idea," Valentino persisted. "We'll start in Gemelli with you traveling around to some of the orange groves. With a farming background that dates back close to a century, you'll be the perfect person to talk to the owners."

Valentino could tell by the way Vincenzo smiled at Carolena that he loved the idea. His friend said, "After you've finished there, we'll have you do the same thing here in Arancia with our lemon farmers. We'll put the video on television in both countries. People will say, 'That's the beautiful Signorina Baretti advertising the AG logo.' You'll be famous."

She shook her head. "I don't want to be famous."

"You get used to it," Valentino quipped. "While you're in Gemelli, you'll stay at the palace and have full security when you travel around with the film crew.

I'll clear my calendar while you're there so I can be on hand. The sooner we get started, the better. How long will it take you to put your affairs in order and fly down?"

"But—"

"It'll be fun," Abby spoke up with enthusiasm. "I can't think of another person who could do this."

"Naturally you'll be compensated, Carolena," Vincenzo added. "After coming to the aid of our two countries, you'll make enough money to buy back your grandparents' farm, if that's what you want."

She got up from the chair on the pretense of getting herself another helping of food. "You're all very flattering and generous, but I need time to think about it."

Valentino stared up at her. "Do that while you're at the symphony tonight with your date, and we'll contact you in the morning for your answer." He could swear she didn't really have plans. She proved it when she looked away from him.

Forcing himself to calm down, he checked his watch. "Since we have several hours before you have to leave in the limo, I suggest we get to work on a script. Perhaps the video could start with you showing us your old farm. It will capture everyone's interest immediately. We'll shoot that segment later."

"It's a beautiful place!" Abby cried. "You'll do it, right?" she pleaded with her friend. "You've worked nonstop since law school. It's time you had some fun along with your work. Your boss, Signor Faustino, will get down on his knees to you."

Vincenzo joined in. "I'll have you flown down on the jet."

Valentino found himself holding his breath.

You go where angels fear to tread, Carolena.

The words pummeled her as the royal jet started its descent to Gemelli's airport. As she saw the smoke of Etna out of the window, memories of that glorious day and evening with Valentino clutched at her heart.

She'd be seeing him in a few minutes. If this offer to do the video had been Valentino's wish alone, she would have turned him down. But the excitement and pleading coming from both Abby and Vincenzo two days ago had caused her to cave. Deep down she knew a great deal was riding on this project for their two countries.

After another sleepless night because of Valentino, she'd phoned Abby the next morning to tell her she'd do it. But her friend had no idea of her fatal attraction to him.

It *was* fatal and Valentino knew it. But he was bound by a code of honor and so was she. If she worked hard, the taping could be done in a couple of days and she could go back to Arancia for good.

One of Valentino's staff greeted the plane and walked her to her old room, where she was once again installed. He lowered her suitcase to the parquet floor. "In forty-five minutes His Highness will be outside in the limo waiting to take you for a tour of some orange groves. In the meantime, a lunch tray has been provided for you."

"Thank you."

After quickly getting settled, she ate and changed

into jeans and a blouson, the kind of outfit she used to wear on her grandparents' farm. Earlier that morning she'd put her hair in a braid to keep it out of her way. On her feet she wore sensible walking boots. Inside her tote bag she carried a copy of the script, which she'd read over many times.

Before walking out the door, she reached for it and for her grandmother's broad-brimmed straw hat she'd always worn to keep out the sun. Armed with what she'd need, she left the room for the limo waiting out at the side entrance of the palace.

When she walked through the doors, Valentino broke away from the driver he'd been talking to and helped her into the limo. The sun shone from a blue sky. It was an incredible summer day. Once inside, he shut the door and sat across from her wearing a navy polo shirt and jeans. He looked and smelled too marvelous for words.

Within a minute they left the palace grounds and headed for the outskirts of the city. "I've been living for you to arrive," he confessed in his deep voice. "How was the symphony?"

His unexpected question threw her. "Wonderful."

"That's interesting. I found out it wasn't playing that night, nor did you go to dinner with your boyfriend. In case you were wondering, the limo driver informed Vincenzo you told him to take you back to your apartment. Why manufacture an excuse?"

Heat rushed to her face. "I'm sure you know the reason."

"You mean that you were afraid you might end up alone with me that evening?"

"I thought it could be a possibility and decided to err on the side of caution."

"Once I overheard Vincenzo tell Abby about your fictional evening out, you don't know how close I came to showing up at your apartment that night."

This wasn't going to work. The longing for him made her physically weak. "Does your mother know you flew me up on Etna?" she blurted.

"She has her spies. It's part of the game. That's why I didn't attack you on the deck of the yacht."

"But we danced for a long time."

He leaned forward. "Dancing is one thing, but the steward would have told her I didn't spend the night with you. In fact, I wasn't in your room more than a few minutes."

"She's no one's fool, Val."

"What can I say?" He flashed her a brief smile. "She's my mother. When she thought you'd gone out of my life by flying back to Arancia with Abby and Vincenzo, no doubt she was relieved. But now that you're here again so soon, she knows my interest in you goes deeper than mere physical attraction."

"With your marriage looming on the horizon, she has every right to be upset."

"That's a mother's prerogative. For that, I apologize."

Valentino's life truly wasn't his own. Every move he made was monitored. Only now was she beginning to appreciate how difficult it must have been for him growing up, but she couldn't worry about that right now. She had a job to do. The sooner she got to it, the sooner she could fly back to Arancia. *Away from him.*

The surrounding countryside basked under a heavenly sun. They came to the first grove where the trees were planted in rows, making up football-pitch-length orchards. She watched men and women in blue overalls go from tree to tree, quickly working their way up and down ladders to fill plastic crates with the brightly colored produce. It brought back memories from her past.

The limo pulled to a stop. "We'll get out and walk from here."

He opened the door to help her. With a shaky hand she reached for her hat. The moment she climbed out, the citrus smell from the many hectares of orange groves filled her senses.

Valentino's dark blue eyes played over her face and figure with a hunger that brought the blood to her cheeks. When she put the hat on her head, he felt the rim of it. "I like that touch of authenticity."

"It was my grandmother's. I thought I'd wear it to bring me luck." Maybe it would help her to keep her wits. But already she was suffering from euphoria she shouldn't be feeling. It was because they were together again. For a while, happiness drove away her fears as they began walking toward the *masseria,* the typical farmhouse in the area.

"As you can see, the groves here have a unique microclimate provided by the brooding volcano of Etna. Warm days and cool nights allow us to produce what we feel are the best blood oranges in the world."

"You ought to be the one on the video, Val. I can hear your love of this island in your voice."

"Yet anyone will tell you a beautiful woman is much more exciting to look at."

Not from her vantage point. Valentino was drop-dead gorgeous. Abby had said as much about Michelina's older brother before Carolena had ever even seen a picture of him.

Several of the security men went on ahead to bring the grove owner to her and Valentino. The man and his son were delighted to be interviewed and would have talked for hours. No problem for them to be part of the video.

After saying goodbye, they drove on to the next orange grove, then the next, stopping for a midafternoon lunch brought from the palace kitchen. Six stops later they'd reached the eastern end of the island. Already it was evening. They'd been so busy, she hadn't realized how much time had passed.

Carolena gave him a covert glance. "There wasn't one farmer who didn't want to be a part of your plan to keep people on the farms and grow more profits."

He sat back in the seat looking relaxed, with his arms stretched out on either side of him. "You charmed everyone. Being a farmer's daughter and granddaughter got them to open right up and express their concerns. I marveled at the way you were able to answer their questions and give them the vision of what we're trying to do."

"I had a script. You didn't. Give yourself the credit you deserve, Val. They fell over themselves with joy to think their prince cares enough about the farmers to honor them with a personal visit. Securing their future secures the entire country and they know it."

"I believe Vincenzo and I are onto something, Carolena, and you're going to be the person who puts this marketing strategy over. After a hard day's work, this calls for a relaxing dinner. I've told the driver to take us to a restaurant here on the water where we can be private and enjoy ourselves. I called ahead to place our order."

This was the part she was worried about. "I think we should go back to the palace."

"You're worrying about my mother, but since she's been worrying about me since I turned sixteen, it's nothing new. I hope you're hungry. We're going to a spot where the *tunnacchiu 'nfurnatu* is out of this world. The tuna will have been caught within the last hour."

It was impossible to have a serious talk with Valentino right now. After they'd eaten, then she'd speak her mind.

The limo pulled down a narrow alley that led to the back entrance of the restaurant he'd been talking about. Valentino got out first and reached for her hand. He squeezed it and didn't let go as he led them to a door one of the security men opened for them.

Cupping her elbow, he walked her down a hallway to another door that opened on to a small terrace with round candlelit tables for two overlooking the water. But they were the only occupants. She shouldn't have come to this romantic place with him, but what could she do?

The air felt like velvet, bringing back memories of their night on the yacht. A profusion of yellow-and-orange bougainvillea provided an overhang Carolena found utterly enchanting.

He helped her to be seated, then caressed her shoulders. She gasped as his touch sent a white-hot message through her. "I've been wanting to feel you all day." Between the heat from his body, plus the twinkling lights on the water from the other boats, she sensed the fire building inside her.

"Benvenuto, Valentino!" An unfamiliar male voice broke the silence, surprising Carolena.

Valentino seemed reluctant to remove his hands. "Matteo Tancredi, meet my sister-in-law's best friend, Carolena Baretti. Carolena, Matteo is one of my best friends and the owner of this establishment."

"How do you do, *signor.*" She extended her hand, hoping his friend with the broad smile and overly long brown hair didn't notice the blush on her face.

"I'm doing very well now that Valentino is here. He told me he was coming with the new star of a video that is going to make Gemelli famous."

She shook her head. "Hardly, but we're all hoping this venture will be a success."

"Anything Valentino puts his mind to is certain to produce excellent results." She heard a nuance of deeper emotion in his response. Still staring at her, he said, "I'll bring some white wine that is perfect with the fish. Anything you want, just ask."

"Thank you."

The two men exchanged a private glance before Matteo disappeared from the terrace. Valentino sat down opposite her. A slight breeze caused the candle to flicker, drawing her attention to his striking features. She averted her eyes to stop making a feast of him.

"Where did you meet Matteo?"

"At the college in Catania."

"Is he married?"

"Not yet. He was studying geology when his father took ill and died. The family needed Matteo to keep this place running, so he had to leave school."

"Wasn't there anyone else to help?"

"His mother and his siblings, but his father always relied on Matteo and didn't like the idea of him going to college."

"Matteo's the eldest?"

"Yes."

"Like the way your father relied on you rather than your younger brother?"

He stared at her through shuttered eyes. "Yes, when you put it that way."

"I can see why. After watching you as you talked with the farmers today, I think you should be the one featured on the film, Val. You're a natural leader."

Before she could hear his response, Matteo brought them their dinner and poured the wine. "Enjoy your meal."

"I'm sure it's going to taste as good as it smells. I think I'm in heaven already," she told him.

"Put it in writing that you were in heaven after eating the meal, and I'll frame it to hang on the wall with the testimonials of other celebrities who've eaten here. But none of them will be as famous as you."

Gentle laughter fell from her lips. "Except for the prince, who is in a category by himself."

"Agreed."

"What category is that?" Valentino asked after Matteo had left them alone.

"Isn't it obvious?" She started eating, then drank some wine.

He picked at his food, which wasn't at all like him. "For one night can't you forget who I am?" Suddenly his mood had turned darker and she felt his tension.

Over the glass, she said, "No more than you can. We all have a destiny. I saw you in action today and am so impressed with your knowledge and caring, I can't put it into words. All I know is that you should be the one featured on the video, not me.

"There's an intelligence in you that would convince anyone of anything. First thing tomorrow, I'm flying back to Arancia while you get this video done on your own. Then your mother will have no more reason to be worried."

His brows furrowed in displeasure. "Much as she would like you to be gone, you can't do that."

"Why not?"

"Because you're under contract to Vincenzo and me." As if she could forget. "The economic future of our two countries is resting on our new plan of which you are now an integral part."

She fought for breath. "But once I've finished the other video session in Arancia, then my work will be done. Just so you understand, I'm leaving Gemelli tomorrow after the filming and won't be seeing you again."

"Which presents a problem for me since I never want you out of my sight. Not *ever*," he added in a husky whisper.

She couldn't stop her trembling. "Please don't say things like that to me. A relationship outside a royal engagement or marriage could only be a tawdry, scandalous affair, so why are you talking like this?"

"Because I'm obsessed with you," he claimed with primitive force. "If it's not love, then it's better than love. I've never been in love, but whatever this feeling is, it's not going away. In fact, it's getting worse, much worse. I'm already a changed man. Believe me, this is an entirely new experience for me."

Incredulous, she shook her head. "We hardly know each other."

"How long did it take you to fall in love with your fiancé?"

She let out a small cry. "How did you find out I had a fiancé?"

"Who else but Abby."

"I wish she hadn't said anything."

"You still haven't answered my question."

"Berto and I were friends on neighboring farms before we fell in love. It's not the same thing at all."

"Obviously not. At the swimming pool last week you and I experienced a phenomenon as strong as a pyroclastic eruption. It not only shook the ground beneath us *before* we were up on the volcano, it shook my entire world so much I don't know myself anymore."

"Please don't say that!" She half moaned the words in panic.

"Because you know it's true?" he retorted. "Even if you weren't the perfect person to do this video for us, I would have found another means to be with you. I've given you all the honesty in me. Now I want all your honesty back. Did you agree to do this video because you wanted to help and felt it was your duty because of your friendship with Abby? Or are you here because you couldn't stay away from me?"

She buried her face in her hands. "Don't ask me that."

"I have to. You and I met. It's a fact of life. Your answer is of vital importance to me because I don't want to make a mistake."

"What mistake? What on earth do you mean?"

"We'll discuss it on the way back to the palace. Would you care for dessert?"

"I—I couldn't." Her voice faltered.

"That makes two of us."

When Matteo appeared, they both thanked him for the delicious food. He followed them out to the limo where they said their goodbyes.

Once inside, Valentino sat across from her as they left the restaurant and headed back to the city. He leaned forward. "Tell me about your fiancé. How did he die?"

She swallowed hard. "I'd rather not get into it."

"We're going to have to." He wasn't about to let this go until he had answers.

"Th-there was an accident."

"Were you with him when it happened?"

Tears scalded her eyelids. "Yes."

"Is it still so painful you can't talk about it?"

"Yes."

"Because you made it happen."

"Yes," she whispered.

"In what way?"

Just remembering that awful day caused her lungs to freeze. "I was helping him with his farm chores and told him I would drive the almond harvester while he sat up by the yellow contraption. You know, the kind that opens into a big upside-down umbrella to catch all the almonds at once?"

"I do. More almonds can be harvested with fewer helpers."

She nodded. "He said for me to stay back at the house, but I insisted on driving because I wanted to help him. I'd driven our family's tractor and knew what to do. We'd get the work done a lot faster. Berto finally agreed. As we were crossing over a narrow bridge, I got too close to the wall and the tractor tipped. Though I jumped out in time, he was thrown into the stream below.

"The umbrella was so heavy, it trapped his face in six inches of water. He couldn't breathe—I couldn't get to him or move it and had to run for help. By the time his family came, it was too late. He'd...drowned."

In the next second Valentino joined her on the seat and pulled her into his arms.

"I'm so sorry, Carolena."

"It was my fault, Val. I killed him." She couldn't stop sobbing.

He rocked her for a long time. "Of course you didn't. It was an accident."

"But I shouldn't have insisted on driving him."

"Couldn't he have told you no?"

She finally lifted her head. Only then did he realize she'd soaked his polo shirt. "I made it too difficult for him. My grandmother told me I could be an impossible child at times."

Valentino chuckled and hugged her against his side. "It was a tragic accident, but never forget he wanted you with him because he loved you. Do you truly believe he would have expected you to go on suffering over it for years and years?"

"No," she whispered, "not when you put it that way."

"It's the only way to put it." His arms tightened around her. "Abby told me he was the great love of your life."

No. Abby was wrong. Berto had been her *first* love. Until his death she'd thought he'd be her only love. But the *great* love of her life, the one man forbidden to her, was holding her right now. She needed to keep that truth from him.

"As I told you before, I'll always love Berto. Forgive me for having broken down like that."

CHAPTER FIVE

VALENTINO KISSED HER hair. "I'm glad you did. Now there are no more secrets between us." Before Carolena could stop him, he rained kisses all the way to her mouth, dying for his first taste of her. She turned her head away, but he chased her around until he found the voluptuous mouth he'd been aching for.

At first she resisted, but he increased the pressure until her lips opened, as if she couldn't help herself. He felt the ground shake beneath him as she began to respond with a growing passion he'd known was there once she allowed herself to let go.

Because they were outside the entrance and would need to go in shortly, he couldn't do more than feast on her luscious mouth. His lips roved over each feature, her eyelids, the satin skin of her throat, then came back to that mouth, giving him a kind of pleasure he'd never known before.

They kept finding new ways to satisfy their burning longing for each other until he didn't know if it was his moan or hers resounding in the limo. *"Carolena—"* he cried in a husky voice. "I want you so badly I'm in pain."

"So am I." She pulled as far away from him as she could. "But this can't go on. It should never have happened. Have you told Vincenzo about me?"

"No."

"I'm thankful for that. After being on the yacht with you, I suppose this was inevitable. Maybe it's just as well we've gotten this out of our system now."

He buried his face in her neck. "I have news for you, *bellissima*. You don't get this kind of fire out of your system. It burns hotter and hotter without cessation. Now that I know how you feel about me, we need to have a serious talk about whether I get married or not."

Her body started to tremble. *"What did you say?"*

"You heard me. I made a vow to myself and my mother there'd be no more women, and I meant it. So what just happened between us means an earthshaking development has taken place we have to dea—"

"Your Highness?" a voice spoke over the mic, interrupting him. "We've arrived."

Carolena let out a gasp. "I can't get out yet. I can't let the staff see me like this—"

He smiled. "There's no way to hide the fact that you've been thoroughly kissed. How can I help?"

"Hand me my bag so I can at least put on some lipstick."

"You have a becoming rash, all my fault."

She groaned. "I can feel it. I'll have to put on some powder."

"Your bag and your hat, *signorina*. Anything else?"

"Don't come near me again."

"I'm accompanying you to your apartment. Are you ready?"

"No." She sounded frantic. "You get out first. I'll follow in a minute."

"Take your time. We're not in a hurry." He pressed another hot kiss to her swollen lips before exiting the limo a man reborn. This had to be the way the captive slave felt emerging from his prison as Michelangelo chipped away the marble to free him.

In a minute she emerged and hurried inside the palace. Valentino trailed in her wake. He followed her into her apartment and shut the door. But he rested against it and folded his arms.

"Now we can talk about us in total privacy."

She whirled around to face him. "There *is* no us, Val. If you were a mere man engaged to a woman you didn't love, you could always break your engagement in order to be with a person you truly care about. In fact, it would be the moral thing to do for both your sakes."

"I hear a but," he interjected. "You were about to say that since I'm a prince, I can't break an engagement because it would be immoral. Is that what you're saying?"

A gasp escaped her lips. "A royal engagement following a royal betrothal between two families who've been involved for years is hardly the same thing."

"Royal or not, an engagement is an engagement. It's a time to make certain that the impending marriage will bring fulfillment. My sister hoped with all her heart the marriage to Vincenzo would bring about that magic because she loved him, but he wasn't in love with her and it never happened."

"I know. We've been over this before," Carolena said in a quiet voice. "But you made a vow to yourself and your family after your uncle Stefano's death. I agreed to come to Gemelli in order to help you and Vincenzo. I—I rationalized to myself that our intense attraction couldn't go anywhere. Not with your wedding dawning.

"But now for you to be willing to break your engagement to be with me is absolutely terrifying. You've helped me to get over my guilt for Berto's death, but I refuse to be responsible for your breakup with Princess Alexandra. You made a promise—"

"That's true. I promised to fulfill my royal duty. But that doesn't mean I have to marry Alexandra. After what you and I shared a few minutes ago, I need more time. Day after tomorrow parliament convenes. You and I have forty-eight hours before my wedding is officially announced to the media. *Or not.*"

If he was saying what she thought he was saying...

"You're scaring me, Val!"

"That's good. On the yacht you had the power to keep me from your bed, which you ultimately did. Your decision stopped us from taking the next step. But tonight everything changed.

"Whatever your answer is now, it will have eternal consequences for both of us because you know we're on fire for each other in every sense of the word. Otherwise you would never have met with me and Vincenzo to discuss our project in the first place. Admit it."

She couldn't take any more. "You're putting an enormous burden on me—"

"Now you know how *I* feel."

"I can't give you an answer. You're going to be king in seven weeks!"

"That's the whole point of this conversation. There'll be no coronation without a marriage. I'll need your answer by tomorrow night after the taping here is finished. Once parliament opens its session the next morning and the date for my wedding is announced, it will be too late for us."

Carolena was in agony. "That's not fair!"

His features hardened. "Since when was love ever fair? I thought you found that out when your fiancé died. I learned it when my sister died before she could hold her own baby."

Tears ran down her cheeks once more. "I can't think right now."

"By tomorrow evening you're going to have to! Until then we'll set this aside and concentrate on our mission to put Gemelli and Arancia on the world map agriculturally."

"How can we possibly do that? You've done a lot more than proposition me. I can hardly take it in."

"That's why I'm giving you all night to think about it. I want a relationship with you, Carolena. I'm willing to break my long-standing engagement to Princess Alexandra in order to be with you. In the end she'll thank me for it. Gemelli doesn't need a king yet."

"You can't mean it!"

"Had I not told you of my engagement, we would have spent that night on the yacht together. But the fact that I *did* tell you proved how important you were to me. I realized I wanted much more from you than one night of passion beneath the stars. Sleeping together to slake our desire could never be the same thing as having a full relationship."

His logic made so much sense she was in utter turmoil.

"However, there is one thing I need to know up front. If your love for Berto is too all consuming and he's the one standing in the way of letting me into your life, just tell me the truth right now. If the answer is yes, then I swear that once this video is made, I'll see you off on the jet tomorrow night and our paths will never cross again."

She knew Valentino meant what he said with every fiber of his being. He'd been so honest with her, it hurt. If she told him anything less she'd be a hypocrite.

"I would never have wanted to sleep with you if I hadn't already put Berto away in my heart."

"That's what I thought," he murmured in satisfaction.

"But when you speak of a relationship, we're talking long-distance. With you up on the volcano while I'm in court in a different country... How long could it last before you're forced to give me up and find a royal bride in order to be king? Your mother would despise me. Abby would never approve, nor would Vincenzo. The pressure would build until I couldn't stand the shame of it."

His eyes became slits. "Do you love me? That's all I want to know."

Carolena loved him, all right. But when he ended it— and he'd be the one to do it—she'd want to die. "Love isn't everything, Val."

"That's not what I wanted to hear, Carolena."

"I thought you gave me until tomorrow evening for my answer."

"I made you a promise and I'll keep it. Now it's getting late. I'll say good-night here and see you at eight in the morning in this very spot. *Buona notte,* Carolena."

Valentino was headed for his suite in the palace when his brother came out of the shadows at the top of the stairs wearing jeans and a sport shirt instead of his uniform. "Vito? What are you doing here? I didn't know you were coming!"

They gave each other a hug. "I've been waiting for you."

Together they entered his apartment. "I take it you've been with mother."

"*Sì.* She phoned me last week and asked me to come ASAP." Valentino had a strong hunch why she'd sent for her second son. "I arranged for my furlough early and got here this afternoon."

"It's good to see you." They sat down in the chairs placed around the coffee table. "How long will you be here?"

"Long enough for me to find out why our mother is so worried about you. Why don't you tell me about the woman you took up on the volcano last week before you spent part of the night dancing with her on the yacht. And all this happening *after* you'd set the date for your marriage to Alexandra."

Valentino couldn't stay seated and got out of the chair. "Do you want a beer?"

"Sure."

He went in the kitchen and pulled two bottles out of the fridge. After they'd both taken a few swallows, Vito said, "I'm waiting."

"I'm aware of that. My problem is finding a way to tell you something that's going to shock the daylights out of you."

With a teasing smile, Vito sat back in the chair and put his feet up on the coffee table. "You mean that at the midnight hour, you suddenly came upon the woman of your dreams."

Valentino couldn't laugh about this. "It was evening, actually. I'd just come from the helicopter. Carolena was in the swimming pool ready to take a dive."

"Aphrodite in the flesh."

"Better. Much better." The vision of her in that bathing suit never left him. He finished off the rest of his beer and put the empty bottle on the table.

"Abby's best friend, I understand. Did I hear mother right? She's helping you and Vincenzo with a marketing video?"

He took a deep breath. "Correct." Valentino explained the project to his brother.

"I'm impressed with your idea, but you still haven't answered my question." Vito sat forward. "What is this woman to you? If word gets back to Alexandra about your dining and dancing with her on the yacht, you could hurt her a great deal."

Valentino stared hard at his brother, surprised at the extent of the caring he heard in his voice. "For the first time in my life I'm in love, Vito."

"You?"

He nodded solemnly. "I mean irrevocably in love."

The news robbed his brother of speech.

"I can't marry Alexandra. There'll be no wedding or coronation in August, no announcement to Parliament."

Color left Vito's face before he put his bottle down and got to his feet. He was visibly shaken by the news.

"Until I met Carolena, I deluded myself into thinking Alexandra and I could make our marriage work by having children. Now I realize our wedding will only doom us both to a life of sheer unhappiness. I don't love her and she doesn't love me the way Michelina loved Vincenzo.

"Despite what our parents wanted and planned for, *I* don't want that kind of marriage for either of us. Tomorrow evening I'm planning to fly to Cyprus and break our engagement. The news will set her free. Hopefully she'll find a man she can really love, even if it causes a convulsion within our families."

Somehow he expected to see and hear outrage from his brother, but Vito did neither. He simply eyed him with an enigmatic expression. "You won't have to fly there. Mother has invited her here for dinner tomorrow evening."

His brows lifted. "That doesn't surprise me. Under the circumstances, I'm glad she'll be here. After I see Carolena off on her flight back to Arancia, I'll be able to concentrate on Alexandra."

"What are you planning to do with Carolena? You can't marry her, and Mother doesn't want to rule any longer."

Valentino cocked his head. "I'm not the only son.

You're second in line. All you'd have to do is resign your commission in the military and get married to Princess Regina. Mother would step down so you could rule. As long as one of us is willing, she'll be happy."

"Be serious," he snapped. "I'm not in love with Regina."

His quick-fire response led Valentino to believe his brother was in love with someone else. "Who is she, Vito?"

"What do you mean?"

"The woman you *do* love." His brother averted his eyes, telling Valentino he'd been right about him.

"Falling in love has totally changed you, Val."

"It has awakened me to what's really important. Carolena makes me feel truly alive for the first time in my life!"

Vito shook his head in disbelief. "When am I going to meet her?"

"The next time I can arrange it."

"When will you tell Mother you're breaking your engagement?"

"After I've talked to Alexandra and we've spoken to her parents. Will you meet the princes at the plane for me? Carolena and I will be finishing up the filming about that time. You'd be doing me a huge favor."

His brother blinked like someone in a state of shock. "If that's what you want." When he reached the door to leave, he glanced around. "Val? Once you've broken with Alexandra, you can't go back."

"I never wanted the marriage and have been putting it off for years. She hasn't pushed for it, either. We're both aware it was the dream of both sets of parents. I've always liked her. She's a lovely, charming woman who deserves to be loved by the right man. But I'm not that man."

After a silence, "I believe you," he said with puzzling soberness.

"A domani, Vito."

The film crew followed behind the limo as they came to the last orange grove. Carolena looked at the script one more time as the car pulled to a stop, but the words swam before her eyes. The hourglass was emptying. Once this segment of the taping was over, Valentino expected an answer from her.

Though he hadn't spoken of it all day, the tension had been building until she felt at the breaking point. She couldn't blame the hot sun for her body temperature. Since last night she'd been feverish and it was growing worse.

After reaching for her grandmother's sun hat, she got out of the limo and started walking down a row of orange trees where the photographer had set up this scene with the owner of the farm and his wife.

Her braid swung with every step in her walking boots. She felt Valentino's eyes following her. He watched as one of the crew touched up her makeup one more time before putting the hat on her head at just the right angle. She'd worn jeans and a khaki blouse with pockets. Casual yet professional.

Once ready, the filming began. Toward the end of the final segment, she held up a fresh orange to the camera. "Eating or drinking, the blood orange with the AG stamp brings the world its benefits from nature's hallowed spot found nowhere else on earth." She let go with a full-bodied smile. "*Salute* from divine Gemelli."

Valentino's intense gaze locked onto hers. *"Salute,"* he murmured after the tape stopped rolling and they started walking toward the limo. "The part you added at the end wasn't in the script."

Her heart thudded unmercifully. "Do you want to redo it?"

"Anything but. I've always considered Gemelli to be 'nature's hallowed spot.' You could have been reading my mind."

"It's hard not to. As I've told you before, you show a rare reverence for the island and its people."

As he opened the limo door for her, the rays of the late-afternoon sun glinted in his dark blond hair. "Your performance today was even more superb than I had hoped for. If this video doesn't put our message across, then nothing else possibly could. I'm indebted to you, Carolena. When Vincenzo sees the tape, he'll be elated and anxious for the filming to start in the lemon groves of Arancia."

"Thank you." She looked away from him and got in the limo, taking pains not to brush against him. Once he climbed inside and sat down opposite her, she said, "If we're through here, I need to get back to the palace."

"All in good time. We need dinner first. Matteo has not only lent us his boat, he has prepared a picnic for us to eat on board. We'll talk and eat while I drive us back." Despite having dinner plans that night, Val decided spending time with Carolena on her last night was too important to miss. He would make arrangements to see Princess Alexandra at the palace afterward.

Carolena had this fluttery feeling in her chest all the way to the shore, where they got out and walked along the dock to a small cruiser tied up outside the restaurant. There would be no crew spying on them here. His security people would be watching them from other boats so they could be strictly alone.

Throughout the night Carolena had gone back and forth fighting the battle waging inside her. By morning she knew what her answer would be. But right now she was scared to death because he had a power over her that made her mindless and witless.

While Valentino helped her on board and handed her a life jacket to put on, Matteo appeared and greeted them. The two men chatted for a minute before Val's friend untied the ropes and gave them a push off. Carolena sat on a bench while Valentino stood at the wheel in cargo pants and a pale green sport shirt.

After they idled out beyond the buoys, he headed into open calm water. Having grown up on an island, he handled the boat with the same expertise he exhibited in anything he did.

She saw a dozen sailboats and a ferry in the far distance. High summer in the Mediterranean brought the tourists in droves. Closer to them she glimpsed a few small fishing boats. Most likely they were manned by Valentino's security people.

When they'd traveled a few miles, he turned to her.

"If you'll open that cooler, I'll stop the engine while we eat."

Carolena did his bidding. "Your friend has made us a fabulous meal!" Sandwiches, salad, fruit and drinks. Everything they needed had been provided. Because of nerves, she hadn't been hungrier earlier, but now she was starving. By the way his food disappeared, Valentino was famished, too.

When they couldn't eat another bite, she cleaned things up and closed the lid. "Please tell Matteo the food was wonderful!" She planned to send him a letter and thank him.

Valentino took his seat at the wheel, but he didn't start the engine or acknowledge what she'd said. "Before we get back, I want an answer. Do I call off the engagement so you and I can be together without hurting anyone else? I haven't touched you on purpose because once I do, I won't be able to stop."

The blood pounded in her ears. She jumped to her feet and clung to the side of the boat. The sun had dropped below the horizon, yet it was still light enough to see the smoke from Etna. Everywhere she looked, the very air she breathed reminded her of Valentino. He'd changed her life and she would never be the same again.

But her fear of being responsible for someone else wasn't the only thing preventing her being able to answer him the way he wanted. Already she recognized that if she got too close to him, the loss she would feel when she had to give him up would be unbearable. To be intimate with him would mean letting him into her heart. She couldn't risk that kind of pain when their affair ended. An affair was all there could ever be for them.

If she left Gemelli first thing in the morning and never saw him again, she'd never forget him, but she'd convinced herself that by not making love with him, she could go on living.

"It's apparent the answer is no."

His voice sounded wooden, devoid of life. It cut her to the quick because she knew that by her silence she'd just written her own death sentence.

Slowly she turned around to face him. His features looked chiseled in the semidarkness. "I saw the light in every farmer's eyes when they talked with you. They were seeing their future king. Putting off your wedding and coronation to be with me won't change your ultimate destiny.

"But you were right about us. What we felt at the pool was like a pyroclastic eruption. They don't come along very often. I read that there are about five hundred active volcanoes on earth, and fifteen hundred over the last ten thousand years. That's not very many when you consider the span of time and the size of our planet. You and I experienced a rare phenomenon and it was wonderful while it lasted, but thank heaven it blew itself out before we were consumed by its fire. No one has been hurt."

"No one?" The grating question fell from the white line of his lips. She watched his chest rise and fall visibly before he made a move to start the engine.

In agony, Carolena turned and clung to the side of

the boat until he pulled into a dock on palatial property some time later.

A few of his staff were there to tie it up. After she removed her life jacket, Valentino helped her off the boat and walked her across the grounds to her apartment. By the time they reached her door, her heart was stuck in her throat, making her feel faint.

"I'm indebted to you for your service, Carolena. Tomorrow my assistant will accompany you to the helicopter at seven-thirty. He'll bring your grandmother's hat with him. Your jet will leave at eight-fifteen from the airport."

Talk about pain…

"Thank you for everything." She could hardly get the words out.

His hooded blue eyes traveled over her, but he didn't touch her. *"Buon viaggio, bellissima."*

When he strode away on those long, powerful legs, she wanted to run after him and tell him she'd do anything to be with him for as long as time allowed them. But it was already too late. He'd disappeared around a corner and could be anywhere in the palace by now.

You had your chance, Carolena. Now it's gone forever.

CHAPTER SIX

"ABBY?"

"Carolena—thank heaven you called! Where are you?"

"I'm back at the office."

"You're kidding—"

"No." Carolena frowned in puzzlement.

"I thought you'd be in Gemelli longer."

"There was no need. I finished up the video taping last evening. I'm pleased to say it went very well. This morning I left the country at eight-fifteen. When the jet landed in Arancia, I took a taxi to my apartment and changed clothes before coming to the firm. It's amazing how much work can pile up in a—"

"Carolena—" Abby interrupted her, which wasn't like her.

She blinked. "What's wrong?"

"You don't know?" Her friend sounded anxious.

"Know what?" She got a strange feeling in the pit of her stomach.

"Vincenzo's source from Gemelli told him that the queen opened parliament this morning without Valentino being there and no announcement was made about his forthcoming marriage. Parliament only convenes four times a year for a week, so the opportunity has been missed."

Carolena came close to dropping her cell phone.

"When you were with him, did he tell you anything? Do you have any idea what has happened?"

"None at all." It was the truth. Carolena could say that with a clear conscience. "When the taping was over last evening, we returned to the palace with the camera crew and I went straight to bed once I got back to my apartment."

She had no clue where Valentino had gone or what he'd done after he'd disappeared down the hall. But if he had been in as much turmoil as Carolena... She started to feel sick inside. "This morning I had breakfast in my room, then his assistant took me to the helicopter at seven-thirty and wished me a good flight. I know nothing."

"It's so strange. Vincenzo has tried to get through to him on his cell phone, but he's not taking calls. Something is wrong."

"Maybe he decided to announce it at the closing."

"I said the same thing to my husband, but he explained it didn't work that way. Any important news affecting the country is fed to the media early on the first day for dissemination."

"Maybe Valentino and the princess decided to postpone their wedding for reasons no one knows about. From what I've seen of him, he's a very private person."

"You're right, but over the last year he and Vincenzo

have grown close. My husband is worried about him. Frankly, so am I."

That made three of them.

Carolena gripped the phone tighter. She'd told Valentino a relationship with him wouldn't work, so if he'd decided to call off the wedding, then he did it for reasons that had nothing to do with her. She refused to feel guilty about it, but she'd grown weak as a kitten and was glad she was sitting down.

"I'm sure he'll get back to Vincenzo as soon as he can. Do you think it's possible there was some kind of emergency that required his presence at the volcanology lab in Catania?"

"I hadn't even thought of that. I'll ask Vincenzo what he thinks."

For all Carolena knew, Val had returned the boat to Matteo where he could confide in his friend in private before parliament opened. But like Vincenzo, she was getting more anxious by the minute.

"Did I tell you Valentino had a copy made of the video? His assistant brought it to me. I've got it right here and will courier it to the palace so you and Vincenzo can see what you think."

"I have a better idea. Come to the palace when you're through with work. We'll have a light supper and watch it. Maybe by then Vincenzo will have heard from him. I take it you haven't seen the video yet."

"No, and I have to tell you I'm nervous."

"Nonsense. I'll send the limo for you at five o'clock. Max will be excited to see you."

"That little darling. I can't wait to hold him." The

baby would be the distraction she needed. But until quitting time, she had a stack of files to work through.

"*Ciao,* Abby."

Three hours later Abby greeted her at the door of their living room, carrying Max in her arms. His blue sunsuit with a dolphin on the front looked adorable on him. "If you'll take the video, I'll tend him for a while." Then, to the little boy, "You remember me, don't you?"

She kissed one cheek then the other, back and forth until he was laughing without taking a breath. "Oh, you precious little thing. I can tell you're all better."

In a few minutes Vincenzo joined them. The second Max saw him, he lunged for his daddy. Their son was hilarious as he tried to climb on everything and clutched at anything he could get his hands on.

After they ate dinner in the dining room, Abby put the baby to bed and then they went back to the living room to watch the video. The whole time her hosts praised the film, Carolena's thoughts were on Valentino, who'd been standing next to the cameraman watching her.

Where was he right now? Enough time had gone by for her anxiety level to be off the charts.

When the film was over, Vincenzo got to his feet and smiled at her. "It's outstanding from every aspect, but *you* made it come alive, Carolena."

"It's true!" Abby chimed in.

"Thank you. I enjoyed doing it. The farmers were so thrilled to meet Valentino in person and listen to his ideas, it was really something to watch."

"Tomorrow we'll drive to the lemon groves to set up appointments."

Abby hugged her. "You were fabulous, Carolena! That hat of your grandmother's was perfect on you. I'm sorry she's not alive to see you wearing it."

Carolena would have responded, but Vincenzo's cell phone rang, putting a stop to their conversation. He checked the caller ID, then glanced at them. "It's Valentino. I'll take it in the bedroom." With those words Carolena's heart fluttered like a hummingbird's wings.

Abby let out a relieved sigh. "Finally we'll learn what's going on. If he hadn't called, I was afraid my husband would end up pacing the floor all night. He worries about Queen Bianca, who's had her heart set on this marriage. She really likes Alexandra."

Every time Abby said something, it was like another painful jab of a needle, reminding Carolena of the grave mistake she could have made if she'd said yes to Valentino. Last night had been excruciating. Several times she'd let down her resolve and had been tempted to reach for the phone. The palace operator would put her call through to Valentino. And then what? She shivered. Beg him to come to her room so they could talk?

When she thought she couldn't stand the suspense a second longer, Vincenzo walked into the living room. For want of a better word, he looked stunned. Abby jumped up from the couch and ran over to him. "What's happened, darling?"

He put his arm around her shoulders. "He and Alexandra have called off their marriage."

Valentino had actually done it?

"Oh, no—" Abby cried softly.

"Valentino has spoken with the queen and Alexandra's parents. It's final. He told me he doesn't want to be married unless it's to a woman he's in love with." Carolena felt Vincenzo's searching gaze on her, causing her knees to go weak. Had Valentino confided in him about her?

"Michelina always worried about him," Abby whispered.

Vincenzo looked at his wife. "Evidently, Alexandra feels the same way, so in that regard they're both in better shape than their parents, who've wanted this match for years. He says that after sixteen years of being betrothed, he feels like he's been let out of prison. I'm one person who can relate to everything he said."

Abby hugged him tightly.

"But there's a big problem. Bianca doesn't want to continue ruling, so it will be up to parliament if they'll allow Valentino to become king without a wife. It's never been done, so I doubt it will happen."

"Where's Valentino now?"

"Since Vito is home on leave from the military and wants to spend time with their mother, Valentino is planning to fly here in the morning and finish up our project with Carolena."

The news was too much. Carolena sank into the nearest chair while she tried to take it all in.

"I told him we watched the video and have a few ideas. Apparently he's seen it several times, too, and has some suggestions of his own. We'll ask the nurse to tend Max so the four of us can make a day of it."

By now Carolena's stomach was in such upheaval, she was afraid she was going to be sick. "In that case, I need to leave and study the script we wrote for the filming here before I go to bed. Thanks for dinner. I'll see you tomorrow."

Abby walked her to the door. "I'll phone you in the morning to let you know what time the limo will come for you. It all depends on Valentino." She stared at Carolena. "He's fortunate that Alexandra wasn't in love with him. If Michelina hadn't loved Vincenzo so much, he—"

"I know," Carolena broke in. "But their two situations weren't the same and your husband is an honorable man." What had happened to Valentino's promise to not fail his parents like his uncle Stefano had done?

Abby's eyes misted over. "So is Valentino. Rather than put himself and Alexandra through purgatory, he had the courage to go with his heart. I admire him for that. The volcanologist in him must be responsible for going where others fear to tread. With that quality he'll make an extraordinary king one day when the time is right."

But he wouldn't, not if he followed in his uncle's footsteps.

With those words, Carolena felt her grandmother's warning settle on her like the ash from Mount Etna.

"See you tomorrow, Abby." They hugged.

"There's a limo waiting for you at the front entrance, but before you go, I have to tell you I've never seen you looking more beautiful than you did in that video. There was an aura about you the camera captured, as if you were filled with happiness. Do you know you literally glowed? The sadness you've carried for years seems to have vanished."

It was truth time. "If you're talking about Berto, then you're right. The trip to Gemelli has helped me put the past into perspective. I thank you for that. *Buona notte,* dear friend."

Valentino's jet landed at the Arancia airport the next morning at 7:00 a.m. He told the limo driver waiting for him to drive straight to Carolena's condo building.

At quarter to eight they pulled around the back. He'd arrived here fifteen minutes early on purpose and would get inside through the freight entrance. Abby had told her they'd come for her at 8:00 a.m., but Valentino told Abby he'd pick up Carolena on the way from the airport to save time. They could all meet at the first lemon grove on the outskirts of Arancia at nine.

One of his security people went ahead to show him the way. Though she planned to be outside waiting, he wanted the element of surprise on his side by showing up at her door ahead of time.

The knowledge that he was free to be with her set off an adrenaline rush like nothing he'd ever known. He rounded the corner on the second floor and rapped on the door. A few seconds later he heard her voice. "Who's there?"

Valentino sucked in his breath. "Open the door and find out."

After a silence, *"Your Highness?"* It came out more like a squeak.

"No. My name is Val."

Another silence. "It *is* you."

The shock in her voice made him smile. "I'm glad you remembered."

"Of course I remembered!" she snapped. That sounded like the woman he'd first met. "You shouldn't have come to my condo."

"Why not? Circumstances have changed."

"They haven't where I'm concerned." Her voice shook.

"That's too bad because the pyroclastic eruption you thought had blown itself out was merely a hiccup compared to what's happening now."

"I can't do this."

"Neither of us has a choice."

"Don't say that—"

"Are you going to let me in, or do I have to beg?"

"I—I'm not ready yet," she stammered.

"I've seen you in a bathrobe before." The sight of her had taken his breath.

"Not this time!"

The door opened, revealing a fully dressed woman in a peasant-style white blouse and jeans. Her long sable hair, freshly shampooed, framed a beautiful face filled with color. With those green eyes, she was a glorious sight anytime. "Please come in. I need to braid my hair, but it will only take me a minute." She darted away.

He shut the door. "I'd rather you left it long for me," he called after her before moving through the small

entrance hall to her living room. It had a cozy, comfortable feel with furnishings that must have belonged
to her family. Lots of color in the fabric. Through the
French doors he glimpsed a book-lined study with a
desk and computer.

"I'm afraid it will get too messy."

Valentino had expected that response and wandered
around the room. There was a statue on an end table
that caught his eye. On close examination it turned out
to be a reproduction of Rodin's *The Secret.* The sculpture of two white marble hands embracing could have
described both the evocative and emotive nature of his
experience with Carolena.

He found it fascinating she would have chosen this
particular piece. There was an intimacy about it that
spoke to the male in him. She was a woman of fire.
He'd sensed it from the beginning and wanted to feel
it surround him.

Next, he saw some photographs of her with a man in
his early twenties, their arms around each other. This
had to be Berto. They looked happy. The loss would
have been horrendous in the beginning.

On one of the walls was a large framed photograph
of a farmhouse. No doubt it was the one she wanted to
buy back one day. His gaze dropped to the table below
it, where he was able to look at her pictures compris-
ing several generations.

"I'm ready."

He picked up one of them. "Your parents?" He
showed the photo to her.

"Yes."

"There's a strong resemblance to your mother. She was beautiful."

"I agree," she said in a thick-toned voice.

"What happened to them?"

Her eyes filmed over. "Mother could never have another child after me and died of cervical cancer. A few years later my father got an infection that turned septic and he passed away, so my grandparents took over raising me. Later on, my grandfather died of pneumonia. He worked so hard, he just wore out. Then it was just my grandmother and me."

He put the picture down and slid his hands to her shoulders. "You've had too much tragedy in your young life."

Her eyes, a solemn green, lifted to his. "So have you. Grandparents, an uncle, a sister and a father gone, plus a kingdom that needs you and will drain everything out of you…"

Valentino kissed her moist eyelids. "You're a survivor, Carolena, with many gifts. I can't tell you how much I admire you."

"Thank you. The feeling is mutual, but you already know that." She'd confined her hair in a braid, which brought out the classic mold of her features.

"I came early so we could talk before we meet Vincenzo and Abby."

He could feel her tension as she shook her head and eased away from him. "Even though you've broken your engagement to Princess Alexandra, which is a good thing considering you don't love her, what you've done changes nothing for me. I don't want an affair with you,

Val. That's all it would be until you have to marry. After your uncle's death, you made that promise to yourself and your parents, remember?"

"Of course." He put his hands on his hips. "But I want to know about you. What do *you* want?"

The grandfather clock chimed on the quarter past. "It's getting late." She walked to the entrance hall.

Valentino followed her. "I asked you a question."

She reached for her straw bag on the credenza. "I want to finish this taping and get back to my law practice."

He planted himself in front of the door so she couldn't open it. "Forget I'm a prince."

Her jaw hardened. "That's the third time you've said that to me."

"What would you want if I weren't a prince? Humor me, Carolena."

He heard her take a struggling breath. "The guarantee of joy in an everlasting marriage with no losses, no pain."

That was her past grief talking. "As your life has already proved to you, there is no such guarantee."

Her eyes narrowed on him. "You *did* ask."

"Then let me add that you have to grab at happiness where you find it and pray to hold on to it for as long as possible."

"We can't. You're a prince, which excludes us from taking what we want. Even if you weren't a prince, I wouldn't grab at it."

His face looked like thunder. "Why not?"

"It—it's not important."

"The hell it isn't."

"Val—we need to get going or Abby and Vincenzo will start to worry."

"The limo is out in the back, but this conversation isn't over yet." He turned and opened the door. After their stops at the various farms, they would have all night tonight and tomorrow night to be together, not to mention the rest of their lives. "I brought your hat with me, by the way."

"Thank you. I would hate to have lost it."

He escorted her out to the limo. With the picture of the marble statue still fresh in his mind, he reached for her hand when they climbed into the car. He held on to it even though he sat across from her. The pulse at her wrist was throbbing.

"Was the Rodin statue a gift from Berto?"

"No. I found it in a little shop near the Chapelle Matisse in Vence, France, with my grandmother. I was just a teenager and we'd gone to France for the week-end. She didn't care for the sculpture, but I loved it and bought it with my spending money. I don't quite know why I was so taken with it."

"I found it extraordinary myself. It reminded me of us. Two would-be lovers with a secret. With only their hands, Rodin's genius brought out their passion." He pressed a kiss to the palm of hers before letting it go.

"I don't like secrets."

"Nor I, but you're being secretive right now."

"Now isn't the time for serious conversation."

"There'll be time later. Vincenzo has planned our itinerary. The farmer at the first grove speaks Mentonasc, so Abby is going to be our translator. She won't want to be in the video, but when we start taping tomorrow, Vincenzo and I are depending on you to get her in it. A blonde and a brunette, both beauties, will provide invaluable appeal."

"You're terrible," she said, but he heard her chuckle. Some genuine emotion at last.

"Matteo told me about the special bottle of Limoncello you express mailed to him from Arancia to thank him for the picnic. The man was very touched, especially by your signature on the label with the five stars next to it."

"You have a wonderful friend in him."

"He has put it up on the shelf behind the counter where all the customers will see it. When your video is famous, he will brag about it. Before we got off the phone he asked me to thank you."

"That was very nice of him." Before long they arrived at the first lemon grove. "It looks like we've arrived."

"Saved by the bell," he murmured.

Praying the others wouldn't look too closely at her, Carolena got out of the limo. It was a good thing the filming wouldn't be until tomorrow. If she'd had to deal with the crew's makeup man, he would know she felt ill after making her exit speech to Valentino.

To her relief, Abby was already talking to the farmer and his two sons. Being fluent in four languages made her a tremendous asset anytime, but Carolena could tell this farming family was impressed that Prince Vincenzo's wife could speak Mentonasc.

He introduced everyone. She could tell the family was almost overcome in the presence of two princes, but Abby had a way of making them feel comfortable while she put her points across. Before long, the four of them left to move on to the next grove. Carolena would have stayed with Abby, but Valentino cupped her elbow and guided her to their limo.

"We all need our privacy," he murmured against her ear after they got back in the car. He acted as though they'd never had that earlier conversation. Even though he sat across from her, being this close to him caused her to be a nervous wreck. His half smile made him so appealing, it was sinful.

"It's a good thing I'll be along tomorrow, too. The younger men couldn't take their eyes off of you. I'm going to have to guard you like a hawk."

In spite of how difficult it was to be alone with him, she said, "You're very good on a woman's ego."

"Then you can imagine the condition my ego is in to be the man in your life. In feudal times they'd have fought me for you, but they'd have ended up dying at the end of a sword."

"Stop—"

He leaned forward, mesmerizing her with those dark blue eyes. "I *am* the man in your life. The only man."

A shudder passed through her body. "I won't let you be in my life, and I can't be the woman in yours. When the taping is over, we won't be seeing each other again."

"Then you haven't read your contract carefully."

Her pulse raced in alarm. "I didn't sign a contract."

"You did better than that. You gave me and Vincenzo

your word. That's as good as an oath. Implicit in the contract is your agreement to deliver the videos and fly-ers with the AG logo to the fruit distributors around the country. We'll go together. It'll take at least a week. For-tunately my brother will be around to help my mother."

Aghast, she cried, "I can't be gone from the firm that long."

"Vincenzo already cleared it with Signor Faustino. Day after tomorrow we'll fly back to Gemelli to begin our tour. By then the tapes and flyers will be ready. I haven't had a vacation in two years and am looking forward to it."

She could see there was no stopping Valentino. Fear and exhilaration swept over her in alternating waves. "What about your work at the geophysics center?"

"I'm long overdue the time off. You're stuck with me. For security's sake, we'll sleep on the yacht at night and ferry across to the island by helicopter during the day. Don't worry. I won't come near you, not after you made your thoughts clear to me."

"You promise?"

He sat back. "I promise not to do anything you don't want me to do. It'll be all business until this is over."

"Thank you." She knew he would keep his promise. The only problem was keeping the promise to herself to keep distance between them.

"Our last stop tomorrow will be the Baretti farm. Judging from the photograph in your living room, the house has a lot of character."

"I loved it, but I don't want us to bother the new owners."

"We won't. You let us know when to stop and the cameraman will take some long shots while you talk about life on the farm growing up. When the film is spliced, we'll start the video with your visit. Will it be hard to see it again?"

Her heartbeat sped up. "I don't know."

"We don't have to do that segment if you decide against it."

"No. I'd like to do it as a tribute to my family." Emotion had clogged her throat.

"I'm glad you said that because I long to see the place where you grew up. I want to learn all about you. The first tree you fell out of, your first bee sting."

Valentino was so wonderful she could feel herself falling deeper and deeper under his spell. "I know about the putti but have yet to learn which staircase at the palace was your first slide. No doubt you spent hours in the Hall of Arms. A boy's paradise."

"Vito and I had our favorite suits of armor, but we put so many dents in them, they're hardly recognizable."

"I can't imagine anything so fun. My friends and I fought our wars in the tops of the trees throwing fruit at each other. The trouble we got into would fill a book. My grandmother would tell you I was the ring-leader. And you were right. I did fall out of a tree several times."

His low chuckle warmed her all the way through and set the tone for the day. She had to admit it was heaven to be with him like this. Carolena needed to cherish every moment because the time they spent together would be coming to an end too soon.

Eight hours later when she was alone back at her condo, she called Abby's cell phone, desperate to talk about what was happening to her.

"Carolena?"

"Sorry to bother you." She took a deep breath. "Are you free?"

"Yes. The baby's asleep and I'm in the bedroom getting ready for bed. Vincenzo and Valentino are in the study talking business. Everything went so well today, they're both elated and will probably be up for another couple of hours. What's wrong?"

She bit her lip. "I'm in trouble."

"I *knew* it."

"What do you mean?"

"You and Valentino. Vincenzo and I watched you two that first night while we were having dinner when he couldn't take his eyes off you. You're in love."

No—

"My husband was certain of it when Valentino took you up on Mount Etna. You're the reason he called off his wedding."

"Don't say that, Abby! We haven't fallen in love. He's just infatuated. You know… forbidden fruit. It'll pass."

"He's enjoyed a lot of forbidden fruit over the years, but he never ended it with Alexandra until he met you."

"That's because he was with me the night his mother insisted on setting the wedding date. When confronted with the reality, it made him realize he can't marry a woman he doesn't love. *That* I understand. But it wasn't because of me. All I did was serve as the catalyst."

"Are you only infatuated, too?"

"What woman wouldn't be?" she cried in self-defense. "Unfortunately he's the first man since Berto to attract me, but I'll get over it."

After a pause. "Have you—"

"No!" she defended.

"Carolena, I was only going to ask if you two had talked over your feelings in any depth."

"Sorry I snapped. We've talked a little, but I'm afraid of getting too familiar with him." She'd come so close to making love with him.

"I've been there and know what you're going through. Let's face it. No woman could resist Valentino except a strong woman like you. He's temptation itself. So was Vincenzo. You'll never know how hard it was to stay away from him."

"Yes, I do. I lived through that entire experience with you. But my case is different. Please try to understand what I'm saying. Everything came together to lay the groundwork for the perfect storm because that's all it is. A perfect storm."

"Then what's the problem?"

"He wants me to fly down to Gemelli the day after tomorrow and spend a week distributing all the marketing materials with him. I—I can't do it, Abby."

"If you're not in love with him, then why can't you go? He has employed you to do a job for him."

"How can you of all people ask me that? Don't you remember after the baby was born? Your father hid you and was ready to fly you back to the States to get you away permanently from Vincenzo so there'd be no hint of scandal."

"But Vincenzo found me and proposed."

"Exactly. Your situation was unique from day one. Vincenzo was married to a princess before he married you. You carried his baby and the king made an exception in your case because he could see his son was in love with you. It's not the same thing at all with Valentino and me. He only *thinks* he's in love."

"So he's already gone so far as to tell you how he feels?"

She swallowed hard. "Like I said, I'm a new face, but certainly not the last one. Be honest, Abby. Though he never loved Alexandra, he'll have to find another royal to marry. In the meantime, if people see me with him, they'll link me with his broken betrothal and there really will be a scandal. I don't want to be known as the secret girlfriend who caused all the trouble."

Her statue of *The Secret* had taken on a whole new meaning since morning. She'd never look at it again without remembering the way he'd kissed her in the limo.

"What trouble? No one knows about you."

"No one except the entire palace staff, his best friend on the island, his colleagues at the volcanology institute in Catania *and* his mother. By the time we've traveled all around the island, the whole country will have seen us together. The queen doesn't want me back in Gemelli."

"Valentino loves her, but he makes his own decisions. If he wants you there, she can't stop him except to bring pressure to bear on you."

"What should I do?"

"I'm the last person to ask for advice."

"Do it anyway. I trust your judgment."

"Well, if I were in your shoes, I believe I'd give myself the week to honor my commitment to him. In that amount of time you'll either lose interest in each other or not. No one can predict the future, but while you're still under contract, do your part. Maybe it will help if you treat him like the brother you and I always wished we'd had."

A brother...

CHAPTER SEVEN

"VAL? SINCE WE'RE already on the eastern side of the island, why don't we stop for dinner at Matteo's restaurant before we fly back to the yacht." She wanted people
around them and thought the suggestion pleased him.

"I'll call ahead and see what can be arranged."

Matteo looked happy to see them, but the place was
busy and they could only chat for a moment with him.
After another delicious dinner, she hurried out to the
limo with Valentino, anxious to leave. They headed for
the heliport on the eastern end of the island. Within a
few minutes they were flying back to the yacht.

In three days they'd covered a lot of territory. He'd
stuck to business while they'd dispensed the videos and
flyers. When they were in the limo, he sat across from
her and there was no touching beyond his helping her
in and out of the car.

Each night she'd pleaded fatigue to keep her distance
from him. To her surprise, he'd told her he, too, was
tired and didn't try to detain her before she went to her
cabin. Instead, he'd thanked her for a wonderful job

and wished her a good night's sleep. She was a fool to wish that he wasn't quite so happy to see her go to bed.

The queen's spies would find no fault in him. His behavior abated Carolena's fears that the time they were forced to spend together on this project would make her too uncomfortable. In truth, she discovered she was having fun doing business with him. He knew so much about the economics that ran his country, she marveled. With others or alone, they had fascinating conversations that covered everything including the political climate.

Valentino remained silent until they'd climbed out of the helicopter. "We need to talk. Let's do it in the lounge before you go to bed."

She walked across the deck with him. When they entered it, she sat down on one of the leather chairs surrounding a small table.

"Would you like a drink?"

"Nothing for me, thank you."

He stood near her, eyeing her with a sober expression. "What were you and Matteo talking about while I took that phone call from Vito?"

Carolena had known he'd ask that question. "He... wanted to know if you'd broken your engagement. I told him yes."

"What else did he say?"

She couldn't handle this inquisition any longer. "Nothing for you to worry about. He's not only a good friend to you, he's incredibly discreet." She looked away to avoid his piercing gaze. "He reminds me of Abby in the sense that I'd trust her with my life."

Valentino studied her until she felt like squirming.

"Do you feel the same about me? Would you trust me with your life?"

The question threw her. She got up from the chair. "I'm surprised you would ask that when you consider I went up on the volcano with you. I'll say good-night now." It was time to go to bed.

"I'd still like a more in-depth answer." The retort came back with enviable calm. "Tell me what you meant earlier when you said you wouldn't grab at happiness even if I weren't a prince?"

"Do I really have to spell it out for you?"

"I'm afraid you do." His voice grated.

She eyed him soberly. "I don't want to be in love again and then lose that person. I've been through it once and can't bear the thought of it. Call me a coward, but it's the way I'm made.

"Whatever you do with the rest of your life, I don't want to be a part of it. As I told you on the yacht the night I thought I would be sleeping with you, I'll never forget how you made me feel, but that's a happy memory I can live with and pull out on a rainy day.

"To have an affair now is something else again. I couldn't do it with you or any man because it would mean giving up part of myself. And when the affair was over, I wouldn't be able to stand the pain of loss because I know myself too well."

He rubbed the back of his neck. "Thank you for your answer. It's all making sense now. Just so you know, I'll be flying to the palace early in the morning."

She was afraid to ask him why, in case he felt she was prying.

"You can sleep in, though I don't know another female who needed her beauty sleep less than you. The steward will serve you breakfast whenever you want it."

"Thank you."

"After I return at ten, we'll do our tour of the south end of the island."

His comment relieved her of the worry that he wouldn't be gone long. Already she missed him, which was perfectly ridiculous.

"After work we'll take the cruiser to a nearby deserted island where we'll swim and watch the wildlife. It's a place where we ought to be able to see some nesting turtles. If it were fall we'd see the flamingos that migrate there on their way to and from Africa. You should see it before you fly back to Arancia."

"I can't wait."

"Neither can I. You'll love it. *A domani.*"

Valentino knocked on Vito's bedroom door early the next morning. His brother was quick to open it wearing a robe. He needed a shave and looked as if he hadn't had any sleep. "What was so urgent I needed to fly here this early?"

Dark shadows below Vito's eyes testified that his younger brother was in pain. "Thanks for getting here so fast. Come on in."

He'd never seen Vito this torn up, not even after Michelina's death. "I take it this isn't about Mother. What's wrong?" He moved inside and followed him into the living room.

Vito spun around, his face full of too many lines for

a thirty-year-old. "I have a confession to make. After you hear me out, I'll understand if you tell me to get the hell out of your life."

Valentino's brows furrowed. "I'd never do that."

"Oh, yes, you would. You will." He laughed angrily. "But I can't keep this to myself any longer." His dark brown eyes filled with tears. "Do you want to know the real reason I went into the military five years ago?"

"I thought it was because you wanted to, and because our father said you were free to do what you wanted."

He shook his dark head. Vito resembled their mother. "What I wanted was Alexandra."

A gasp came out of Valentino. Those words shook him to the foundations.

"I fell in love with her. I don't know how it happened. It just did."

Valentino knew exactly how it happened. He knew it line and verse.

"All the years you were betrothed, you were hardly ever around, and when you were, it was only for a day. Whereas I spent a lot of time with her. One night things got out of control and I told her how I felt about her. We went riding and she told me she was in love with me, too. We ended up spending the weekend together knowing we could never be together again."

"*Vito—*"

"You were betrothed to her, and the parents had another woman picked out for me, so I left to join the military with the intention of making it my career for as long as possible. I was a coward and couldn't face you, but I should have."

Pure unadulterated joy seized Valentino. He didn't need to hear another word. It suddenly made sense when he remembered his brother occasionally telling him things about Alexandra that surprised Valentino. It explained the huge relief he saw in Alexandra's eyes when he'd called off the marriage. But what he'd thought was relief was joy.

In the next breath he gave his brother the biggest bear hug of his life, lifting him off the ground. "You're more in love with her than ever, right?"

Vito staggered backward with a look of disbelief in his eyes. "Yes, but how come you're acting like this? You have every right to despise me."

He shook his head. "Nothing could be further from the truth. If anything, I've been the despicable one for not ending it with Alexandra years ago. I knew something earthshaking had happened to make you go away. I was afraid I'd offended you in some way. Now that you've told me, I'm so incredibly happy for you and Alexandra, you could have no idea.

"Don't waste another moment, Vito. All this time you two have been in pain… Give up your commission and marry her. Grab at your happiness! Mother loves her, and her parents want to join our two families together. When they find out you're going to be king instead of me, they'll be overjoyed."

"I don't want to be king."

"Yes, you do. You told me years ago. The point is, *I* don't. I never wanted it."

"But—"

"But nothing," Valentino silenced him. "Mother is

perfectly healthy. Maybe she's going to have to rule for a lot longer than she'd planned."

His brother rubbed the back of his neck in confusion. "What's going on with you? Do I even know you?"

He grinned. "We're brothers, and I've got my own confession to make, but you'll have to hear it later. In the meantime, don't worry about me. And don't tell Mother I've been to the palace this morning. I'll be back in a few days." He headed for the door and turned to him. "When I see you again, I'd better hear that you and Alexandra have made your wedding plans or there *will* be hell to pay."

Valentino flew out the door and raced across the grounds to the helicopter. The knowledge that Vito and Alexandra had been lovers had transformed him, removing every trace of pain and guilt.

"Carolena?"

She peered around the deck chair where she'd been reading a magazine in her sunglasses. "Hi!"

This morning she'd put her vibrant hair back in a chignon and was wearing pleated beige pants with a peach-colored top her figure did wonders for. Between her sensational looks and brilliant mind, she was his total fantasy come to life.

"If you're ready, we'll get business out of the way, then come back and take off for the island." He'd told one of the crew to pack the cruiser with everything they'd need if they wanted to spend the night there.

Throughout the rest of the day they'd gotten things down to a routine and touched base with the many heads of fruit consortiums in the district. The plan to market the island's blood oranges under the AG logo had already reached the ears of many of them with rave results.

Valentino had demands for more of the videos made in Gemelli than he'd anticipated. He gave orders to step up production of the flyers, too. Two more days and he and Carolena would have covered the whole country. By this time next year he'd know if their efforts had helped increase their exports around the world and produced financial gains.

As he'd told Carolena, there were no guarantees in life. This plan of his and Vincenzo's to help their countries' economies was only one of many. It was far too early to predict the outcome, but since she'd come into his life, he had this feeling something remarkable was going to happen.

With their marketing work done, Valentino drove the cruiser under a late-afternoon sun along a string of tiny deserted islands with rocky coastlines.

Carolena had been waiting for this all day. "What's that wonderful smell in the breeze?"

"Rosemary and thyme. It grows wild here among the sand dunes and beaches. Vito and I spent a lot of our teenage years exploring this area. In the fall this place is covered with pink flamingos, herons and storks. We used to camp out here to watch them and take movies."

"I envy you having a brother to go on adventures with. No one's childhood is idyllic, but I think yours must have come close."

"We tried to forget that we were princes put into

a special kind of gilded cage. However, I would have liked your freedom."

"But it wouldn't have exposed you to the world you're going to rule one day. Someone has to do it."

He lifted one eyebrow. "That's one way of looking at it. Ten years ago we worked on our father to get legislation passed in parliament to declare this a natural preserve so the tourists wouldn't ruin it. Since that time, our Gemellian bird-watching society has seen continual growth of the different species, and I've had this place virtually to myself."

She laughed. "Seriously, that has to be very gratifying to you." His dedication to the country's welfare continued to astound Carolena. "This is paradise, Val. The sand is so white!"

He nodded. "It feels like the most refined granulated sugar under your feet. We'll pull in to that lagoon, one of my favorite spots."

The water was as blue as the sky. They were alone. It was as if they were the only people left on earth. After he cut the engine, she darted below to put on her flowered one-piece swimsuit. It was backless, but the front fastened up around the neck like a choker, providing the modesty she needed to be around Val.

When she came back up on deck, she discovered he'd already changed into black trunks. The hard-muscled physique of his bronzed body took her breath. His gaze scrutinized her so thoroughly, he ignited a new fire that traveled through hers.

"Not that the suit you're wearing isn't delectable, but what happened to that gorgeous purple concoction you were wearing when we first met? I've been living to see you in it again."

A gentle laugh broke from her. "You mean that piece of nothing?" she teased. "I've never owned anything indecent before. When I saw it in the shop before I flew down here with Abby, I decided to be daring and buy it. I was a fool to think I'd be alone."

"The sight of you almost in it put an exclamation point on the end of my grueling workday."

She blushed. "*Almost* being the operative word. You're a terrible man to remind me."

"You're a terrible woman to deprive me of seeing you in it again."

Carolena had been trying to treat him like a brother, but that was a joke with the heat building between them. She needed to cool off and there was only one way to do it. She walked to the end of the cruiser and without hesitation jumped into the water.

"Oh—" she cried when she emerged. "This feels like a bathtub! Heaven!"

"Isn't it?"

She squealed again because he'd come right up next to her. They swam around the boat, diving and bobbing like porpoises for at least half an hour. "I've never had so much fun in my life!"

He smiled at her with a pirate's grin that sent a thrill through her. "I'll race you to shore, but I'll give you a head start."

"You're on!" She struck out for the beach, putting everything into it. But when she would have been able to stand, he grabbed hold of her ankles and she landed in the sand. Laughter burst out of her. "That wasn't fair!"

He'd come up beside her and turned her over. "I know," he whispered against her lips. "But as you've found out, I play by a different set of rules. Right now I'm going to kiss the daylights out of you."

"No, Val—" she cried, but the second she felt his hungry mouth cover hers, she couldn't hold off any longer. This time they weren't in the back of the limo while the driver was waiting for them to get out.

There was nothing to impede their full pleasure as they wrapped their arms around each other. Slowly they began giving and taking one kiss after another, relishing the taste and feel of each other. While their legs entwined, the warm water lapped around them in a silky wet blanket.

"You're so beautiful I could eat you alive. I'm in love with you, *adorata*. I've never said it to another woman in my life, so don't tell me it isn't love."

She looked into his eyes blazing with blue fire. "I wasn't going to," she cried in a tremulous whisper before their mouths met in another explosion of desire. Carried away by her feelings, she quit fighting her reservations for the moment and gave in to her longings. She embraced him with almost primitive need, unaware of twilight turning into night.

"I'm in love with you, too, Val," she confessed when he allowed her to draw breath. "I've been denying it to myself, but it's no use. Like I told you on the yacht that first night, you make me feel immortal. Only a man who had hold of my heart could make me thankful I've been born a woman."

He buried his face in her throat. "You bring out feelings in me I didn't know were there. I need you with me, Carolena. Not just for an hour or a day." He kissed her again, long and deep, while they moved and breathed as one flesh.

"I feel the same way," she whispered at last, kissing his jaw where she could feel the beginnings of a beard. No man had ever been as gorgeous.

"Another time we'll come out here in the middle of the night to watch the turtle fledglings hatch and make their trek to the water. Tonight I want to spend all the time we have on the cruiser with you. It's getting cooler. Come on before you catch a chill."

He got up first and pulled her against him. Dizzy from the sensations he'd aroused, she clung to him, not wanting to be separated from him for an instant, but they had to swim back to the boat. Valentino grasped her hand and drew her into the water. "Ready?"

"Yes."

Together they swam side by side until they reached the back of the cruiser. He levered himself in first so he could help her aboard. "You take a shower while I get the cruiser ready for bed. We'll eat in the galley. But I need this first." He planted another passionate kiss on her mouth, exploring her back with his hands before she hurried across the deck and down the steps.

She'd packed a bag with the essentials she'd need. After carrying it into the shower, she turned on the water and undid her hair. It felt marvelous to wash out the sand and have a good scrub. Aware Valentino would want a shower, too, she didn't linger.

Once she'd wrapped her hair in a towel and had dried herself, she pulled out her toweling robe. But when she started to put it on, it was like déjà vu and stopped her cold. What was she doing?

Yes she'd broken down and admitted that she loved him, but nothing else had changed. Though he'd spoken of his love and need to be with her all the time, he was still a prince with responsibilities and commitments she could never be a part of.

Abby had suggested she treat Valentino like a brother in order to make it through the rest of the week, but that tactic had been a total and utter failure. Carolena was painfully, desperately in love with him.

If they made love tonight, her entire world would change. She'd be a slave to her need for him and act like all the poor lovesick wretches throughout time who'd made themselves available to the king when he called for them.

It was sick and wrong! No matter how much she loved Valentino, she couldn't do that to herself. Carolena couldn't imagine anything worse than living each minute of her life waiting for him to reach out to her when he had the time. Once he married and had children, that really would be the end for her.

If she couldn't have him all to herself, she didn't want any part of him. There was no way to make it work. None. She'd rather be single for the rest of her life.

On the yacht that first night she'd told him he'd passed his test and could leave her cabin with a clear conscience. Now it was time for her to pass her test and go away forever.

She quickly put on clean underwear and a new pair of lightweight sweats with short sleeves. The robe she buried in the bottom of the bag. After removing the towel, she brushed her hair back and fastened it at the nape with an elastic.

After putting her bag outside the door, she headed straight into the galley and opened the fridge to get the food set out for them. When she'd put everything on the table, she called to him. A minute later he showed up in a striped robe. He'd just come out of the shower and his dark blond hair was still damp. Talk about looking good enough to eat!

She flashed him a smile. "Is everything fine topside?"

"We're set for the night." His eyes took in her sweats. Carolena knew her friendly air didn't fool him, but he went along with her. "I like your sleepwear. Reminds me of Vito's military fatigues."

"This is as close as I ever hope to get to war," she quipped. "Why don't you sit down and eat this delicious food someone has prepared for us." He did her bidding. She poured coffee for them. "How is your brother, by the way? Will he be in Gemelli long before he has to go back on duty?"

"I don't know." His vague answer wasn't very re-assuring. "He wants to meet you when we get back to the palace."

She bit into a plum. "I'm afraid that won't be possible."

Lines marred his handsome features. "Why would you say something like that? He's my only sibling still alive. Naturally I want him to meet you and get to know you."

"Under normal circumstances there's nothing I'd like more, but nothing about you and me is normal."

His head reared back. "What are you trying to tell me now?"

Carolena eyed him with a frank gaze. "I've already admitted that I'm in love with you, but I've come to my senses since we came back on board and I don't intend to sleep with you tonight or any other night. I want a clean break from you after I've finished out my contract, so there's no need to be involved with any members of your family."

He got that authoritative look. It was something that came over him even if he wasn't aware of it. "There isn't going to be a break."

"So speaks the prince. But this commoner has another destiny. Don't ask me again to forget that you're royalty. It would be pointless. Do you honestly believe I could stand to be your lover in your secret life and watch you play out your public life with a royal wife and children? Other foolish women have done it for centuries, but not me."

Valentino tucked into his pasta salad, seemingly not in the least bothered by anything she'd said.

"Did you hear me?"

"Loud and clear." He kept on eating.

Her anger was kindled. "Stop acting like a husband who's tired of listening to his nag of a wife. Have you ever considered why she nags him?"

"The usual reasons. I had parents, too, remember."

"You're impossible!"

Quiet reigned until he'd finished his coffee. After he put down the mug, he looked at her with those intelligent dark blue eyes. "How would *you* like to be my wife? I already know you have a temper, so I'm not shaking in my boots."

Her lungs froze. "That was a cruel thing to say to me."

His sinuous smile stung her. "Cruel? I just proposed marriage to you and that's the answer you give me?"

Carolena shook her head. "Stop teasing me, Val. Why are you being like this? I thought I knew you, but it's obvious I don't. The only time I see you serious is when you're wearing your princely mantle."

He sat back in the chair. "For the first time in my life, I've taken it off."

She started to get nervous. "Just because you broke your engagement, it doesn't mean you've changed into someone else."

"Oh, but I have!"

"Now you're scaring me again."

"Good. I like it when you're thrown off base. First, let me tell you about my talk with Vito this morning."

Carolena blinked. "That's where you were?"

"He sent me an urgent message telling me he needed to see me as soon as possible. Otherwise I would never have left you."

This had to do with their mother. Guilt attacked her. "Is your mother ill?" she asked.

"No. Last week I told Vito I was breaking my engagement to Alexandra. Since I had business with you,

I asked him to meet the princess's plane when she flew in to Gemelli."

"She came to the palace?"

"That's right. What I didn't know until this morning was that Vito and Alexandra were lovers before he went into the military."

The blood hammered in her ears.

"He signed up intending to make a career of it in order to stay away from her permanently. Neither my parents nor I knew why."

"Those poor things," she whispered.

Valentino nodded. "But after hearing that I'd broken our engagement, he found the courage to face me this morning. To my surprise, I learned she was on the verge of breaking it off with me, but Vito wanted to be the one to tell me. That was why she was so happy that I got there first."

Carolena could hardly take it in. "You mean, they've been in love all these years?"

"Yes. It's the forever kind."

She was dumbstruck.

"When I left Vito, I told him there'd better be a marriage between the two of them soon or he'd have to answer to me. Mother will have no choice but to see him crowned king. The promise that one of her sons will reign makes everything all right. He'll rule instead of me. No one will have to be disappointed, after all."

By now Carolena's whole body was shaking. "Are you saying you'd give up your dream in order to marry me?"

"It was never my dream. My parents thrust the idea upon me as soon as I was old enough to understand."

Dying inside, she got to her feet. "Does your mother know any of this?"

"Maybe by now, which brings me to what I have to say to you. I meant what I said earlier tonight. I want you with me all the time, day and night. Forever." He cocked his head. "Did you mean what you said the other day at your condo when I asked you what *you* wanted?"

Hot tears stung her eyelids. "Yes. But we both concluded it wasn't possible."

"Not both—" He leaned forward and grasped her hand. "I told you that true love had to be grabbed and enjoyed for the time given every mortal. When I asked you to fly up on Etna with me even though you knew there was a risk, you went with me because you couldn't bear to miss the experience."

"That was a helicopter ride. Not a marriage. There can't be one between you and me. You're supposed to be the King!"

"Am I not supposed to have any say in the matter, *bellissima?*"

"Val… You're not thinking clearly."

"I'm a free man, Carolena, and have never known my path better than I do now. When Michelina passed away, Vincenzo was free to marry Abby and he did so in the face of every argument. Lo and behold he's still the prince.

"Whether the government makes him king after his father dies, no one can say. As for me, I'll still be a prince when I marry you. The only difference is, I'll work for Vito after he's crowned."

"You mean *if* he's crowned. Your mother will forbid it."

"You don't know Vito. He wanted Alexandra enough to go after her. It looks like he's got the stuff to make a remarkable king. Once Mother realizes their marriage will save her relationship with Alexandra's parents, she'll come around."

"Does Vito want to be king?"

"I don't think he's given it much thought since everyone thought I'd be the one to assume the throne. But when we were younger and I told him I wanted to be a full-time volcanologist, he said it was too bad I hadn't been born the second son so I could do exactly what I wanted.

"When I asked him what he wanted, he said it might be fun to be king and bring our country into the age of enlightenment. Then he laughed, but I knew he wasn't kidding."

"Oh, Val..."

"Interesting, isn't it? At times, Michelina made the odd remark that he should have been born first. She and I were close and she worried for me always having to do my duty. I worried about her, too. She was too much under the thumb of our parents who wanted her marriage to Vincenzo no matter what."

"If people could hear you talk, they'd never want to trade places with you." She had a tragic look on her beautiful face. "As for your poor mother..."

"She's had to endure a lot of sorrow and disappointment and I'm sorry for that. Naturally I love her very much, but she doesn't rule my life even if she is the queen. I'm not a martyr, Carolena. It turns out Vito isn't, either. To have to marry another royal is archaic to both of us, but in his case he happened to fall in love with one."

"Your mother will think you've both lost your minds."

"At first, maybe. But just because she was pressured into marriage with my father doesn't mean Vito or I have to follow suit. The times have changed and she's being forced to accept the modern age whether she likes it or not. Michelina went through a surrogate to have a baby with Vincenzo. That prepared the ground and has made her less rigid because she loves her grandson."

"But you're her firstborn. She's pinned her hopes on you."

"Haven't I gotten through to you yet? Her hopes aren't mine. When I decided to get my geology degree, she knew I was going to go my own way even if I ended up ruling. After she finds out that Vito wanted to be betrothed to Alexandra years ago instead of me, she's going to see that you can't orchestrate your children's lives without serious repercussions."

"I'm too bewildered by all this. I—I don't know what to say."

"I want you for my wife. All you have to say is yes."

She sank back down in her chair. "No, that isn't all."

"Then talk to me. We've got the whole night. Ask me anything you want."

"Val—it isn't that simple."

"Why not?"

"I—I don't know if I want to be married."

"Because there are no guarantees? We've already had this conversation."

"But that was when we were talking hypothetically."

"Whereas now this is for real?"

She lowered her head. "Yes. For one thing, I don't think I'd make a good wife."

"I've never been a husband. We'll learn together."

"Where would we live?"

"Shall we buy your family's farm and live there?"

Carolena's head flew back. "I would never expect you to move to a different country and do that—your work for the institute is far too important!"

Valentino was trying to read between the lines, but she made it difficult. "I can tell the thought of living at the palace holds little appeal. We'll get our own place."

Her body moved restlessly. "You'd hate it. After a while you'd want to move back."

"There's nothing I'd love more after a hard day's work than to come home to my own house and my own bride. Would you like us to buy a farm here? Or would you prefer working for a law firm in Gemelli?"

She looked tortured. "I don't know." She got up from the chair again. "I can't answer those questions. You haven't even talked to your mother yet. It would be pointless to discuss all this when she doesn't know anything that's gone on with you."

"When we get back to the palace day after tomorrow, we'll go to her and tell her our plans."

"But we don't have any plans!"

He got to his feet. "We love each other and don't want to be separated. That forms the foundation of our

plans. Come to bed with me and we'll work out the lo-
gistics of when and where we want to be married, how
many children we want to have. Do we want a dog?"

"I'm not going to sleep with you."

"Yes, you are. There's only one bed on the cruiser,
but if you ask me not to make love to you, I won't."

After a minute, she said, "You go on ahead. I'll be
there once I've cleaned up the kitchen."

"I'll help. This will get me into practice for when
we're married."

They made short work of it.

"I'll just get ready for bed," Carolena said.

"You do that while I turn out the lights."

She hurried out of the galley. He could tell she was
frightened. Valentino was, too, but his fears were different. If he couldn't get her to marry him, then his life
really wouldn't have any meaning.

Once he'd locked the door at the bottom of the stairs,
he made a trip to the bathroom to brush his teeth. The
cabin was cloaked in darkness when he joined her in
bed still wearing his robe. She'd turned on her side
away from his part of the bed. He got in and stretched
out on his back.

"Val?"

"Yes?"

"Berto and I never spent a night together alone."

His thoughts reeled. "Not even after you were engaged?"

"No. Our families were old-fashioned."

He sat up in bed. "Are you telling me you two never
made love?"

"It was because we didn't want to lie to the priest who'd asked us to wait."

"So you've never been intimate with a man."

"No. After he was killed, I kept asking myself what we'd been waiting for. I know now that a lot of my grief had to do with my sense of feeling cheated. I was so sure another man would never come along and I'd never know fulfillment. It made me angry. I was angry for a long time."

He squeezed her shoulder. "Carolena…"

"Once I started dating, I went through guy after guy the way the tabloids say you've gone through women. But after knowing you for the last week, it all had to have been made up because you don't have that kind of time."

A smile broke the corners of his mouth.

"The fact is, I don't have your experience, but that part doesn't bother me. I just wanted you to know the truth about me. I have no idea if I'd be a satisfying lover or not."

She was so sweet, it touched his heart. "That could work both ways."

"No, it couldn't. When you were kissing me out in the lagoon, I thought I might die on the spot from too much ecstasy." That made two of them. "I'm frightened by your power over me."

His brows knit together. "Why frightened?"

"Because I'm afraid it's all going to be taken away from me."

She'd had too many losses.

"Don't you know I have the same fear? I lost hope

of ever finding a woman I could love body and soul. Yet the moment I was resigned to my fate, I discovered this exquisite creature standing on the diving board of my swimming pool. You've changed my life, Carolena Baretti."

He rolled her into his arms and held her against his body. "I want to be your husband."

She sobbed quietly against his shoulder. "I need more time before I can tell you yes or no. I have too many issues welling up inside of me.

"When I get back to Arancia, I'm going to make an appointment with a professional. I hope someone can help me sort all this out. I should have gone to counseling after Berto died, but I was too wild with pain to even think about it. Instead, I started law school and poured all my energy into my studies."

"How did you end up becoming an attorney?"

"My grandmother insisted I go to college. She said I needed to do something else besides farming in case I had to take care of myself one day. For an old-fashioned woman, she was actually very forward thinking.

"While I was at school studying business, we met with some professors for career day. One of them encouraged me to try for the law entrance exam. I thought why not. When I succeeded in making a high score, the rest was history. Eventually I met Abby and for some reason we just clicked. The poor thing had to listen while I poured out my heart about Berto, but school did help me."

He had to clear the lump in his throat. "Work's a great panacea."

"Yes, but in my case it made me put off dealing with the things that were really wrong with me. Meeting you has brought it all to the surface. I don't want to burden you with my problems, Val. I can't be with you right now. You have to understand that if I can't come to you having worked things out, then it's no good talking about marriage. Please tell me you understand that."

She was breaking his heart. Abby had told him she'd been in a depression for a long time. Carolena reminded him of Matteo, who had certain issues that wouldn't allow him to marry yet.

He clutched her tighter, terrified he was going to lose her. "I do," he whispered into her hair. *I do.* "Go to sleep now and don't worry about anything."

"Please don't say anything to your mother about me. Please," she begged.

"I promise I won't."

"You always keep your promises. I love you, Val. You have no idea how much. But I can't promise you how long it's going to take me before I can give you an answer."

CHAPTER EIGHT

FOUR DAYS LATER the receptionist at the hospital showed Carolena into the doctor's office in Arancia for her appointment.

"*Buongiorno,* Signorina Baretti." The silver-haired psychologist got to his feet and shook her hand before asking her to sit down.

"Thank you for letting me in to see you on such short notice, Dr. Greco. Abby has spoken so highly of you, I was hoping you could fit me in."

"I'm happy to do it. Why don't you tell me what's on your mind."

"I should have come to someone like you years ago."

"Let's not worry about that. You're here now. Give me a little background."

He made a few notes as she started to speak. Pretty soon it all came gushing out and tears rolled down her cheeks. "I'm sorry."

"It's all right. Take your time."

He handed her some tissues, which she used. Finally she got hold of herself. "I don't know what more to tell you."

"I don't need to hear any more. What I've gleaned from everything you've told me is that you have two problems. The biggest one is an overriding expectation of the prince. Because he isn't meeting that expectation, it's preventing you from taking the next step in your life with him."

"Expectation?" That surprised her. She thought she was going to hear that she was losing her mind.

"I find you've dealt amazingly well with everything that's gone on in your past life. But you've got a big problem to overcome, and unless you face it head-on, you'll remain conflicted and depressed."

It was hard to swallow. "What is it?"

"You've just found out the prince wants to marry you. But it means that for your sake he plans to give up his right to sit on the throne one day as king and you don't like that because you've never imagined he could do such a thing. It hasn't been your perception. To some degree it has shocked and maybe even disappointed you, like glitter that comes off a shiny pair of shoes."

Whoa.

"When you were telling me about all the farmers you met who held him in such high esteem, your eyes shone with a bright light. I watched your eyes light up again when you told me how he's preparing the country in case of an eruption on Mount Etna. Your admiration for him has taken a hit to learn he's willing to be an ordinary man in order to be your husband."

"But his whole life has been a preparation for being king."

"Let me put this another way. Think of a knight

going into battle. In his armor astride his horse, he looks splendid and triumphant. But when he takes it off, you see a mere man.

"Your prince is a man first. What you need to do is focus on that."

She kneaded her hands. "Valentino's always telling me to forget he's a prince."

"That's right. The man has to be true to himself. If he had nothing to bring you but himself, would you take him?"

"Yes—" she cried. "He's so wonderful you can't imagine. But what if he marries me and then wishes he hadn't and wants to be king?"

"How old did you say he was?"

"Thirty-two."

"And he called off his wedding to a princess he doesn't love?"

"Yes."

"Then I'd say the man is more than old enough to know his own mind."

"It's just that he already makes a marvelous ruler."

"I thought you said his mother is the ruler."

"Well, she is."

"And he's not the king, so what you're telling me is that he's still marvelous just being a man, right?"

His logic was beginning to make all kinds of sense. "Yes."

"Your other problem is guilt that could be solved by a simple conversation with the queen."

Carolena gulped. "I don't think I could."

"You're going to have to because you're afraid she'll

never forgive you if you marry her son, thus depriving him of his birthright."

Dr. Greco figured all that out in one session? "What if she won't?"

"She might not, but you're not marrying her, and the prince isn't letting her feelings stand in the way of what he wants. It would be nice to have her approval, of course, but not necessary. There's no harm in approaching her and baring your soul to her. She'll either say yes or no, but by confronting her, you'll get rid of that guilt weighing you down."

Valentino had promised he wouldn't talk to his mother about her yet...

"My advice to you is to go home and let this percolate. When you've worked it all out, let me know."

It was scary how fast he'd untangled her fears so she could understand herself. The doctor was brilliant. She jumped to her feet, knowing what she had to do. "I will, Doctor. Thank you. Thank you so very much."

Valentino hunkered down next to Razzi. Both wore gas masks. "Those strombolian explosions are building in intensity."

"You're not kidding. Something big is going on."

He and Razzi had been camped up there for three days taking readings, getting any activity on film. His work kept him from losing his mind. He had no idea how long it would be before he heard from Carolena.

Valentino wasn't surprised to see that a new lava flow had started from the saddle area between the two Southeast Crater cones.

"Look, Razzi. More vents have opened up on the northeast side of the cone."

"There's the lava fountain. It's getting ready to blow."

He gazed in wonder as a tall ash plume shot skyward. Though it was morning, it felt like midnight. Suddenly there were powerful, continuous explosions. The loud detonations that had continued throughout the night and morning sent tremors through the earth.

"We're too close!" The ground was getting too un-stable to stand up. "More lava fountains have started. This is it. Come on, Razzi. We need to move back to the other camp farther down."

They recognized the danger and worked as a team as they gathered their equipment and started their re-treat. He'd witnessed nature at work many times, but never from this close a vantage point.

The continual shaking made it more difficult to move as fast as they needed to. Halfway to the other camp a deafening explosion reached his ears before he was thrust against the ground so hard the impact knocked off his gas mask.

Everything had gone dark. He struggled to find it and put it back on. In frustration he cried to Razzi, but the poisonous fumes filled his lungs. For the first time since coming up on Etna, Valentino had the presenti-ment that he might not make it off the volcano alive.

His last thought was for Carolena, whose fear of an-other loss might have come to pass.

Once Carolena had taken a taxi back to her condo, she made a reservation to fly to Gemelli later in the day.

This was one time she didn't want to burden Abby with her problems.

Officially, Carolena was still out of the office for another week, so she didn't need to make a stop there to talk to Signor Faustino. All she needed to do was pack another bag and take care of some bills before she called for a taxi to drive her to the airport.

The necessity of making all her own arrangements caused her to see how spoiled she'd become after having the royal jets at her disposal. It seemed strange to be taking a commercial jet and traveling in a taxi rather than a limo. Everything took longer. She was tired when she arrived in Gemelli at five-thirty that evening and checked herself into a hotel.

Because she hadn't seen or heard from Valentino for the past four days, she was practically jumping out of her skin with excitement at the thought of being with him again. Her first order of business was to phone the palace. She wanted to surprise him.

After introducing herself to the operator, she asked to speak to Valentino, but was told he was unavailable. The news crushed her. Attempting to recover, she asked if she could speak to Vito Cavelli. Through his brother she could learn Valentino's whereabouts, and possibly he would help her to meet with the queen.

Before long she heard a male voice come on the line. "Signorina Baretti? It's really you?"

"Yes, Your Highness."

"Please call me Vito. You're the famous video star."

"I don't know about famous."

"You are to me. Mother and I have seen the video. It's superb."

"Thank you. I was just going to say that if anyone is renowned, it's you for drawing all those interesting mustaches on the putti around the outside of the palace."

He broke into rich laughter that reminded her so much of Val, she joined in. "Are you calling from Arancia?"

She gripped her phone tighter. "No. I just flew in to Gemelli and am staying at the Regency Hotel."

"*Grazie a Dio* you're here," he said under his breath. His sudden change of mood alarmed her.

"What's wrong?"

"I was hoping you could tell me. Four days ago Valentino left for Catania, but I haven't talked to him since. I've left message after message."

That meant he was working on Etna.

"*Signorina?* Does my brother know you're here?"

"Not yet. I wanted to come to the palace and surprise him."

"Do you have his private cell phone number?"

"Yes. As soon as we hang up, I'll call him."

"Once you've reached him, will you ask him to return my call? I have something important to tell him."

Her brows furrowed. It wasn't like Valentino to remain out of reach. He was too responsible a person to do that. "Vito?"

"*Sì?*"

"There's a favor I'd like to ask of you."

"Name it."

"Would it be possible for me to talk to your mother

either tonight or in the morning? It's of extreme importance to me."

"I'm afraid she's not in the country, but she should be back tomorrow afternoon and then we'll arrange for you to meet with her."

More disappointment. "Thank you. Is she by any chance in Arancia?" Maybe she was visiting Vincenzo and Abby. Carolena should have called her friend, after all.

"No. She flew to Cyprus and left me in charge. I guess Valentino told you about me and Alexandra. The families are together now, discussing our plans to marry. We're thinking in four weeks."

It really was going to happen. "I'm very happy for you, Vito. I mean that sincerely."

"Thank you. I wish I could say the same for my brother."

"What do you mean?"

"It's my impression you're the only person who knows what's going on with him. He's not answering anyone's calls. This is a first for him. Our mother is worried sick about him."

Her eyes closed tightly. Carolena was the one responsible for him shutting down. She took a fortifying breath. "Now that I'm back, I'll try to reach him. Once I've contacted him, I'll tell him to get in touch with you immediately."

"I'd appreciate that. Good luck."

Fear clutched at her heart. Vito knew his brother better than anyone. To wish her luck meant she was going to need it. What if Valentino couldn't call anyone? What if he was in trouble? Her body broke out in a cold sweat.

"Good night, Vito."

"Buona notte, signorina."

As soon as she hung up, she phoned Valentino's number. Forget surprising him, all she got was to leave a message. In a shaky voice she told him she was back in Gemelli, that she loved him and that she was dying to see him. Please call her back.

Crushed because she couldn't talk to him, she got information for Tancredi's Restaurant so she could talk to Matteo. Maybe he'd spoken with Valentino. To her chagrin she learned it was his night off. If she'd like to leave a message... Carolena said no and hung up. The only thing to do was go looking for Valentino.

Again she rang for information and called the airport to schedule a commuter flight for seven in the morning to Catania airport. From there she'd take a taxi to the center where she'd been before. Someone would know how to reach Valentino if he still hadn't returned her call.

She went to bed and set her alarm, but she slept poorly. Valentino still hadn't called her back. At five in the morning she awakened and dressed in jeans and a T-shirt. After putting on her boots, she fastened her hair back in a chignon and left to get some food in the restaurant. Before taking a taxi to the airport, she knew she'd better eat first.

Everywhere she went was crowded with tourists. The commuter flight was packed and she had a long wait at the Catania airport before she could get a taxi to drive her to the institute.

Once she arrived, she hurried inside and approached the mid-twenties-looking man at the reception desk.

He eyed her with male appreciation. "May I help you, *signorina?*"

"I need to get in touch with Valentino Cellini."

The man smiled. "And you are…?"

"Carolena Baretti. I'm an attorney from Arancia who's been working with His Highness on a special project. I have to see him right away."

"I'm afraid that's not possible."

She refused to be put off. "Why not?"

"He's out in the field."

"Then can you get a message to him?"

"You can leave one here. When it's possible for him, he'll retrieve it."

This was getting her nowhere. "Would it be possible to speak to one of the pilots for the center? His name is Dante Serrano. He was the one who recently flew me up on Etna with the prince."

The fact she knew that much seemed to capture his attention. "I'll see if I can locate him." He made a call. After a minute he hung up. "Signor Serrano will be coming on duty within a few minutes."

"In that case, I'll wait for him in the lounge. Will you page me when he gets here?"

"Of course."

"Thank you."

Carolena hadn't been seated long when the attractive pilot walked over to her. She jumped up to greet him, but his expression was so solemn she knew something was wrong.

"Good morning, Dante. I was hoping to talk to you. I haven't been able to reach Valentino."

"No one's been able to reach him or his partner, Razzi. They were camped near a new eruption. The base camp received word that they were on their way back to it, but they lost contact."

"You mean th—"

"I mean, no one has been able to reach them yet."

"Then it must be bad," she cried in agony and grabbed his arms. "I can't lose him, Dante. I can't!"

"Let's not talk about that right now," he tried to placate her. "Half a dozen choppers have already taken off to search for them. This is my day off, but I was called in to help. Valentino's the best of the best, you know."

"I *do* know!" Carolena cried. "My life won't be worth living without him! I'm going with you!"

"No, no. It's too dangerous."

"I *have* to go with you. It's a matter of life and death to me. I love him. We're going to be married."

His eyes rounded before he exhaled a labored breath. "All right. You can come, but you'll do everything I say."

"I promise."

She followed him through the center and out the rear doors to the helipad. They ran to the helicopter. Once she'd climbed inside and strapped herself in the back, he found a gas mask for her. "When I tell you to do it, I want you to put this on."

"I will."

Another pilot joined them. Dante made a quick introduction, then started the engine. The rotors whined. Within seconds they lifted off.

At first, the smoking top of Etna didn't look any different to her. But before long the air was filled with ash. Afraid to disturb Dante's concentration, she didn't dare ask him questions. After ten minutes, the sky grew darker.

As the helicopter dipped, she saw the giant spectacular ash plume coming from a crater filling up with lava. She gasped in terror to think Valentino was down there somewhere.

"Put on your gas mask, *signorina.* We're going to land at the base camp."

She was all thumbs, but finally managed to do it after following his instructions. When they touched ground, Carolena thought there might be thirty geologists in the area wearing gas masks, but visibility was difficult.

"I want you to stay in the chopper until I tell you otherwise." By now he and the copilot had put on their masks.

"I will, but please find him."

"Say a prayer," he murmured. She bowed her head and did exactly that. To lose him now would kill her.

The two men disappeared. In a minute she heard the whine of rotors from another chopper. It set down farther away. People ran to it. She watched in agony as she saw a body being unloaded from it. Valentino's?

Forgetting Dante's advice, she climbed out of the chopper and started running. The victim was being transported on a stretcher to one of several tents that had been set up. She followed and worked her way inside the entrance, but there were too many people around to see anything.

The copilot who'd been on the chopper stood nearby. She grabbed at his arm.

He looked at her. "You weren't supposed to leave the chopper."

"I don't care. Is it Valentino?"

"I don't know yet, but I'll find out."

She held her breath until he came back. "It's Valentino's partner, Razzi."

"Is he…"

"Alive," he answered. "Just dazed from a fall."

"Where's Valentino?"

"The other chopper is bringing him in."

"So they found him!"

"Yes."

Her heart started to beat again. "Thank you for telling me that much." She hurried outside, praying for the other chopper to come.

The next minute felt like an eternity until she heard the sound of another helicopter coming in to land. She hurried over to the area, getting as close as she was allowed until it touched ground.

Carolena watched the door open, but there was no sign of Valentino. She was close to fainting, when Dante pulled her aside. Through his mask he said, "Valentino's head struck some volcanic rock. When they transported him out, he was unconscious but alive."

"Thank heaven." She sobbed quietly against him as they walked toward Dante's chopper.

"You can say that again. He's already been flown to the hospital. I'll fly you there now. Before long you'll be able to visit him."

"Thank you for bringing me up here. I'm indebted to you."

"He's lucky you love him enough to face danger yourself. Not every woman or man has that kind of courage."

She didn't know she had any until she'd been put to the test. It was only because of Valentino. He was her life!

"Razzi said they were eyewitnesses to an explosion that could have gotten them killed. I've heard that the footage they captured on film is the best that's ever been recorded at the institute. The guys are heroes."

They were. "So are you, Dante."

"Yeah?" He smiled.

"Yeah."

Carolena's thoughts drifted back to her conversation with Dr. Greco. He'd said it best. *And he's not the king, so what you're telling me is that he's still marvelous just being a man, right?*

"Your Highness?"

Valentino was lying in bed with his head raised watching television when a nurse came in. He'd been told he had a concussion and would have to stay in the hospital overnight for observation. Much as he wanted to get out of there, every time he tried to sit up, his head swam.

"Yes?"

"Do you feel up to a visitor?"

There was only one person he wanted to see. If she ever came to a decision and it was the wrong one, he wished his body had been left on the side of the volcano.

"Who is it?"

"This person wanted it to be a surprise."

It was probably Vito, who would have been contacted hours ago. He'd want to see Valentino for himself before he told their mother her firstborn was alive and well. But in case it wasn't his brother, Valentino's mind ran through a possible list of friends and colleagues. If it were Vincenzo, he would have just walked in.

"Shall I tell this person you're still indisposed?"

While he was trying to make up his mind, he heard a noise in the doorway and looked up to see Carolena come rushing in the room. "Val, darling—" she blurted in tears and flew toward him.

At the sight of her in a T-shirt and jeans she filled out to perfection, an attack of adrenaline had him trying to get out of bed. But she reached him before he could untangle his legs from the sheet and try to sit up. She pressed against him, wetting his hideous hospital gown with her tears.

"Thank heaven you're alive! If I'd lost you, I would have wanted to die."

He wrapped his arms around her, pulling her up on the bed halfway on top of him. "I'm tougher than that. How did you know I was in here?"

Moisture spilled from her fabulous green eyes. "I flew down to Gemelli last evening. When you didn't answer my call and Vito couldn't get through to you, either. I flew to Catania this morning and took a taxi to the institute."

Valentino was in shock. "You were there this morning?"

"Yes! I had to see you, but then Dante told me you were up on the volcano and there'd been no contact from you since the latest eruption, so I flew up there with him to the base camp."

His blood ran cold. "He took you up there?"

"He wouldn't have, but when I told him you and I were getting married and I couldn't live without you, he took pity on me and let me go with him to look for you."

It was too much to digest. His heart started to act up. "You're going to marry me?"

"As soon as we can." She lifted her hand to tenderly touch his head. "You're my man and I want everyone to know it." In the next breath she covered his mouth with her own. The energy she put into her kiss was a revelation.

"Adorata—" He could believe he'd died on Etna and had just awakened in heaven.

She pressed him back against the pillow and sobbed quietly until the tears subsided. His Carolena was back where she belonged.

"Did you know your mother is in Cyprus seeing about the plans for Vito's wedding to Alexandra? While they have their big day after all they've been through, wouldn't it be thrilling if we had our own private wedding with Vincenzo and Abby for witnesses as soon as possible? I'd love it if we could say our vows in the chapel at the palace.

"And while we're gone on a honeymoon, Vincenzo and Abby could stay at the palace with your mother so she could spend time with Michelina's little boy. I want everyone to be happy. The two of us most of all. What do you think?"

Tears smarted his eyes. She really understood what Valentino was all about. He shaped her face with his hands. "First, I think I want to know what has caused this dramatic change in you."

"A very wise doctor helped me get to the core of what was ailing me. He said I had a fixation on your royal person, which was true. He told me I was disappointed you were willing to forgo being king in order to marry me.

"But my disappointment really covered my guilt over your decision and it made me afraid. Then he asked me if I couldn't love the ordinary man instead of the prince. He said something about looking at you without your crown and battle armor. That question straightened me out in a big hurry and I couldn't get back down here fast enough to tell you."

"Battle armor?" Would wonders never cease? He kissed her lips once more. "Remind me to send the doctor a big bonus check for services rendered."

"I already wrote him one." She ran kisses along his jawline. "You've got a beard, but I like to see you scruffy."

"Maybe I'll let it grow out."

"Whatever you want. Oh—there's just one more thing. The doctor says my guilt will be cured after I've talked to your mother. Even though she'll never forgive me for ruining her dreams for you, I have to confront her."

"We'll do it together tonight."

"But you'll still be in here. The doctor won't release you until tomorrow. We'll talk to her then."

"In that case, come closer and give me your mouth again."

She looked toward the door. "Isn't this illegal? What if someone catches us?"

"Do we care? This is my private room."

"Darling," she whispered, hugging him to her. He was all she ever wanted. "What happened on the volcano? I have to know."

He let out a sigh and rehearsed what went on after the first lava fountain appeared. "When I saw that plume shoot into the atmosphere, I knew we needed to run for our lives."

She gripped him harder. "Were you terrified?"

"Not then. The sight was glorious."

"I saw it from a distance. I don't think there's anything in nature to compare to it."

"There isn't." He rubbed his hands over her back. "Do you remember when you were up there with me the first time and the ground shook?"

Carolena shivered. "I'll never forget."

"Well, try to imagine it so strong, neither Razzi nor I could stand up. That's when it started getting exciting. But the moment came when the force threw me forward. I hit the ground and lost hold of the things I was carrying. Then my gas mask came off."

"Val—"

"That's when I got scared because I couldn't find it in the darkness."

At this point she wrapped her arms around his neck and wept against his chest. "Dante says you're a hero for getting close enough to record the data. I adore you."

His breath caught. "You mean, you're not going to tell me I have to give up my profession?"

She lifted her head. "Are you kidding? Nothing could be more exciting than what you do. I plan to go up with you a lot. When we have children, you can introduce them to the mountain. We'll get the whole family in on the act."

A week later, Carolena sat in front of the same mirror in the same cabin on the yacht brushing her hair. She'd just showered and put on the white toweling robe hanging on the hook in the bathroom.

But there were differences from the first time she'd come down to this room. The first time she'd been on board, the yacht was stationary. Now it was moving. But the gentle waters of the Ionian carried it along like so much fluff. Their destination was the Adriatic. Valentino had mentioned Montenegro as one of their stops. To Carolena, it was all like part of a dream.

Only two hours ago the priest had performed the marriage ceremony in the chapel in front of loved ones and Valentino's best friend, Matteo. On her ring finger flashed an emerald set in white gold. She was now Signora Valentino Agostino Cellini, and she was nervous.

How strange for her to have been so fearless before marriage when she'd thought they were going to make love the first time. Now she really was a bride and her heart thudded with sickening intensity at the thought of it.

A rap on the door caused her to get up jerkily from the dressing table chair. When she turned, she saw that Valentino had slipped into the room wearing a navy robe. He moved toward her, so sinfully handsome her mouth went dry.

"I can tell something's wrong, *bellissima*. I know you missed your parents and grandparents at our wedding. I'd like to think they were looking on and happy. Let me be your family from now on."

It was a touching thing for him to say. She sucked in her breath. "You are. You're my whole life."

His eyes caressed her. "I thought you'd enjoy re-creating our first night on board, but maybe you would have preferred someplace else."

"Never. This is the perfect place."

"As long as you mean it."

"Of course I do."

She didn't know what his intentions were until he picked her up in his arms. "Then welcome to my life, *sposa mia*."

He lowered his mouth to hers and drank deeply as he carried her through the hall to the master suite. After he followed her down on the bed, he rolled her on top of him. "Never was there a more beautiful bride. I realize we've only known each other a short time, yet it seems like I've been waiting for you a lifetime. Love me, Carolena. I need you," he cried with such yearning, she was shaken by a vulnerability he rarely showed.

No longer nervous, her instincts took over and she began loving him. The rapture he created took her to a place she'd never been before. Throughout the night they gave each other pleasure she didn't know was possible.

"Don't ever stop loving me," she begged when morning came around. If they slept at all, she didn't remember. "I didn't know it could be like this, that I could feel like this." She laid against him, studying the curve of his mouth, the lines of his strong features. "I love you, Val. I love you till it hurts. But it's a wonderful kind of hurt."

"I know." He ran his hands through her hair. "Pleasure-pain is ecstasy. We have the rest of our lives to indulge in it to our heart's content." He gave her an almost savage kiss. "To think what we might have missed—"

"I don't want to think about it. Not ever. You set me on fire the first time you looked at me. Not everyone loves the way we do. It's overpowering."

"That's the way it should be when it's right."

She kissed his jaw. "Do you know who looked happy last night?"

"My mother."

Carolena raised up on her elbow. "You saw it, too?"

"She'd never admit it, but deep down she's glad her sons have found true love, something that was denied her."

Her eyes teared up. "After meeting you, I knew she'd always been a great mother, but the accepting way she has handled our news has made me admire her more than you could ever know. I'm growing to love her, Val.

I want to get close to her. She's missing her daughter and I'm missing my grandmother."

He hugged her tighter. "Do you have any idea how much it means for me to hear you say that?"

"It's so wonderful belonging to a family again. To belong to you."

"*You're* so wonderful I can't keep the secret Vincenzo wanted to tell you himself. When he springs it on you, promise me you'll pretend you knew nothing about it."

"They're going to have a baby."

His dark blue eyes danced. "If they are, I don't know about it yet. This particular secret concerns you."

"What do you mean?"

"Instead of handing you a check for invaluable services rendered to both our countries, he approached the latest owner of your grandparents' farm. After some investigation, he learned they're willing to sell it to you, but there's no hurry."

"*Val*— Are you serious?"

He rolled her over on her back and smiled down at her. "I thought that would make you happy. We'll use it as our second home when we fly to Arancia for visits."

"Our children will play in the lemon grove with Abby and Vincenzo's children."

"Yes. And when we get back from our honeymoon, we'll decide where we want to live."

She cradled his handsome face in her hands, loving him to distraction. "It's already been decided by Vito, but it's his secret. You have to promise not to tell him I told you."

His brows quirked. "My brother?"

"Yes. He said he's willing to be king so long as you're close by to help him. To quote him, 'The two Vs stick together.' He's already started a renovation of the un-occupied north wing of the palace where he says you two used to play pirates.

"I found out it has a lookout where you can see Etna clearly. It's the perfect spot for all your scientific equipment. He said the wing will be permanently closed off from the rest of the palace so it will be our own house with our own private entrance."

Her husband looked stunned. "You're okay with that?"

"I love the idea of being close to family. Think how much fun it would be for his children and ours, and they'll have a grandmother close by who will dote on them."

The most beautiful smile imaginable broke out on his face. "Are you trying to tell me you want a baby?"

"Don't you? After last night, maybe we're already pregnant."

"To make certain, I think we'll stay on a permanent honeymoon."

She kissed him until they were breathless. "You were right about the fire, darling. It keeps burning hotter and hotter. Love me again and never stop."

"As if I could…"

* * * * *

Mills & Boon® Hardback
June 2014

ROMANCE

Ravelli's Defiant Bride	Lynne Graham
When Da Silva Breaks the Rules	Abby Green
The Heartbreaker Prince	Kim Lawrence
The Man She Can't Forget	Maggie Cox
A Question of Honour	Kate Walker
What the Greek Can't Resist	Maya Blake
An Heir to Bind Them	Dani Collins
Playboy's Lesson	Melanie Milburne
Don't Tell the Wedding Planner	Aimee Carson
The Best Man for the Job	Lucy King
Falling for Her Rival	Jackie Braun
More than a Fling?	Joss Wood
Becoming the Prince's Wife	Rebecca Winters
Nine Months to Change His Life	Marion Lennox
Taming Her Italian Boss	Fiona Harper
Summer with the Millionaire	Jessica Gilmore
Back in Her Husband's Arms	Susanne Hampton
Wedding at Sunday Creek	Leah Martyn

MEDICAL

200 Harley Street: The Soldier Prince	Kate Hardy
200 Harley Street: The Enigmatic Surgeon	Annie Claydon
A Father for Her Baby	Sue MacKay
The Midwife's Son	Sue MacKay

Mills & Boon® Large Print

June 2014

ROMANCE

A Bargain with the Enemy	Carole Mortimer
A Secret Until Now	Kim Lawrence
Shamed in the Sands	Sharon Kendrick
Seduction Never Lies	Sara Craven
When Falcone's World Stops Turning	Abby Green
Securing the Greek's Legacy	Julia James
An Exquisite Challenge	Jennifer Hayward
Trouble on Her Doorstep	Nina Harrington
Heiress on the Run	Sophie Pembroke
The Summer They Never Forgot	Kandy Shepherd
Daring to Trust the Boss	Susan Meier

HISTORICAL

Portrait of a Scandal	Annie Burrows
Drawn to Lord Ravenscar	Anne Herries
Lady Beneath the Veil	Sarah Mallory
To Tempt a Viking	Michelle Willingham
Mistress Masquerade	Juliet Landon

MEDICAL

From Venice with Love	Alison Roberts
Christmas with Her Ex	Fiona McArthur
After the Christmas Party...	Janice Lynn
Her Mistletoe Wish	Lucy Clark
Date with a Surgeon Prince	Meredith Webber
Once Upon a Christmas Night...	Annie Claydon

0514 GEN STD LP

Mills & Boon® Hardback
July 2014

ROMANCE

Christakis's Rebellious Wife	Lynne Graham
At No Man's Command	Melanie Milburne
Carrying the Sheikh's Heir	Lynn Raye Harris
Bound by the Italian's Contract	Janette Kenny
Dante's Unexpected Legacy	Catherine George
A Deal with Demakis	Tara Pammi
The Ultimate Playboy	Maya Blake
Socialite's Gamble	Michelle Conder
Her Hottest Summer Yet	Ally Blake
Who's Afraid of the Big Bad Boss?	Nina Harrington
If Only...	Tanya Wright
Only the Brave Try Ballet	Stefanie London
Her Irresistible Protector	Michelle Douglas
The Maverick Millionaire	Alison Roberts
The Return of the Rebel	Jennifer Faye
The Tycoon and the Wedding Planner	Kandy Shepherd
The Accidental Daddy	Meredith Webber
Pregnant with the Soldier's Son	Amy Ruttan

MEDICAL

200 Harley Street: The Shameless Maverick	Louisa George
200 Harley Street: The Tortured Hero	Amy Andrews
A Home for the Hot-Shot Doc	Dianne Drake
A Doctor's Confession	Dianne Drake

Mills & Boon® Large Print
July 2014

ROMANCE

A Prize Beyond Jewels	Carole Mortimer
A Queen for the Taking?	Kate Hewitt
Pretender to the Throne	Maisey Yates
An Exception to His Rule	Lindsay Armstrong
The Sheikh's Last Seduction	Jennie Lucas
Enthralled by Moretti	Cathy Williams
The Woman Sent to Tame Him	Victoria Parker
The Plus-One Agreement	Charlotte Phillips
Awakened By His Touch	Nikki Logan
Road Trip with the Eligible Bachelor	Michelle Douglas
Safe in the Tycoon's Arms	Jennifer Faye

HISTORICAL

The Fall of a Saint	Christine Merrill
At the Highwayman's Pleasure	Sarah Mallory
Mishap Marriage	Helen Dickson
Secrets at Court	Blythe Gifford
The Rebel Captain's Royalist Bride	Anne Herries

MEDICAL

Her Hard to Resist Husband	Tina Beckett
The Rebel Doc Who Stole Her Heart	Susan Carlisle
From Duty to Daddy	Sue MacKay
Changed by His Son's Smile	Robin Gianna
Mr Right All Along	Jennifer Taylor
Her Miracle Twins	Margaret Barker

Discover more romance at

www.millsandboon.co.uk

- ❤ WIN great prizes in our exclusive competitions
- ❤ BUY new titles before they hit the shops
- ❤ BROWSE new books and REVIEW your favourites
- ❤ SAVE on new books with the Mills & Boon® Bookclub™
- ❤ DISCOVER new authors

PLUS, to chat about your favourite reads, get the latest news and find special offers:

- Find us on facebook.com/millsandboon
- Follow us on twitter.com/millsandboonuk
- ❤ Sign up to our newsletter at millsandboon.co.uk